The Nebula Awards

This selection of the best science fiction stories of 1969 was chosen by ballot by the Science Fiction Writers of America.

Each of these stories is something special. And together they comprise what has been called the folk literature of the machine age, as they examine the basic elements of human nature in terms of the expansions of science and human awareness.

The single common denominator of these selections is quality. They are entertaining and thought provoking, highly original and imaginative. In short, they are outstanding science fiction.

NEBULA AWARD STORIES FIVE
was originally published by
Doubleday & Company, Inc.

NEBULA
AWARD
STORIES
FIVE

Edited by James Blish

PUBLISHED BY POCKET BOOKS NEW YORK

NEBULA AWARD STORIES FIVE

Doubleday edition published December, 1970

POCKET BOOK edition published January, 1972

This POCKET BOOK edition includes every word contained in the original, higher-priced edition. It is printed from brand-new plates made from completely reset, clear, easy-to-read type. POCKET BOOK editions are published by POCKET BOOKS, a division of Simon & Schuster, Inc., 630 Fifth Avenue, New York, N.Y. 10020. Trademarks registered in the United States and other countries.

L

In Memoriam

ROBERT ARTHUR
EVELYN DEL REY
MRS. DAVID H. KELLER
WILLY LEY
JONQUIL LEIBER
NOEL M. LOOMIS
SEABURY QUINN
JOHN WYNDHAM

CONTENTS

INTRODUCTION

No review of the year 1969 in science fiction (and fantasy, for let us not forget that the membership of the Science Fiction Writers of America voted to embrace this category and admit it to award status) will appear here this year, because I have two invited guests who will be doing that. Instead, I propose to take cognizance of some recent and uninformed criticism of the Nebula Awards system to replace misinformation with facts.

Throughout the year, SFWA members recommend stories they admire to the attention of others through the medium of the group's official organ, the *SFWA Bulletin*. At the end of the year, a nominating ballot is sent out which lists all the stories and novels so recommended. The rules this year say that no story receiving fewer than three recommendations-plus-nominations may appear on the final ballot, and that in any case the number of final nominees in each category (novel, novella, novelet, short story) is restricted to five (although the awards committee may add a sixth to any category if the voting seems close enough to justify it).

Final voting is by Australian ballot; that is, each member indicates his first, second and third choices in each category—he may also vote "abstain" or "no award" in each—and the second and third choices are used only to break ties. The ballots are mailed independently and directly to the New York firm of Walter J. Mathews Associates. The ballots are not signed, but coded, and the numbers are kept confidential. In 1969, too, a major effort was made to supply every member with a copy of each final nominee. (I cannot say how well this effort worked in the United States; in England, I eventually received most of the material, but about a third of what I did get arrived after the voting deadline.) This system may not be tamperproof—I suppose no such system is—but it is fair, and it seems to me that anybody with sufficient ingenuity to rig it successfully is wasting his time, and should be robbing Swiss banks instead.

So much for the mechanics. The objections, which were taken seriously enough to cost us two of our most distinguished members, seemed to center mainly on the allegation that most of the recommendations came from, and most of the awards went to, the members of some small inside group, variously identified with the annual Milford (Pennsylvania) Science Fiction Writers' Conference or "the New Wave writers."

The actual statistics of last year's voting, which were published in the *Bulletin,* made this allegation look extremely dubious. This year's rule it out entirely. The facts are:

A total of 112 nominating ballots were returned, out of a membership of 353 (and I suggest you compare this percentage of returns with the turnout in any national election). One of the novels received *fifty-one* preliminary recommendations; as one of the Milford Conference's three founders, I can tell you that the figure is bigger than the entire working attendance at any Conference since the first one, 'way back in 1954. And I trust nobody can manage to believe that our field contains that many New Wave writers, though Michael Moorcock, who edits and publishes the New Wave's magazine, probably wishes devoutly that it did.

One would think also that a truly effective pressure group ought to be able to hold its lackeys in line between the nominating and the final ballot. It is in fact true that every entry but one which led its category in nominations did go on to win a Nebula, which is what counts, but among the short-listers, the voting pattern shifted markedly. For example, the novel that ran second in number of nominations placed third in the final voting—in fact it received fewer final votes than it had nominations—while the one that had run third changed places with it. Among the novellas, the former second-place runner wound up third, the former *fourth*-place runner placed second, and the former third-place runner dropped out. Among the novelets, the second favorite in the nomina-

10

tions vanished, while the final second and third places were taken by stories which had been tied for third place earlier. The Nebula winner in the short story category had been in a tie for second place in the nominations, while the former favorite wound up in third place.

Finally: six novels won places on the final ballot. I do not yet know how many ballots were returned, but three of these novels—win, place, and show—accumulated 109 votes, so it is obvious that the turnout was even heavier than it had been on the preliminary round, surely equalling and probably passing a third of the active membership.

Of the 109 votes mentioned, a decisive 54 were captured by *The Left Hand of Darkness* (Ace Special/Walker & Co.) by Ursula K. Le Guin. This author, whose *Nine Lives* (which you will find in this book) also took second place in the novelet category, lives in Oregon and has never been to a single Milford Conference.

Slaughterhouse 5 by Kurt Vonnegut, Jr. (Delacorte) came in second with 31 votes. This author did attend one Milford Conference, a fact which he recorded in an earlier novel *(God Bless You, Mr. Rosewater);* but both he and his publishers now insist that he is not a science-fiction writer at all, and he had not been a SFWA member for several years, so his chances of having any sort of claque within SFWA today look vanishingly small.

Norman Spinrad's *Bug Jack Barron* (Avon/Walker) took third place with 24 votes. This book is a New Wave novel by every imaginable test, including that of first publication (in Mr. Moorcock's *New Worlds*), and excited more controversy—with more attendant publicity—than any other novel on the ballot. Mr. Spinrad has also been a frequent and valued attendee of Milford conferences; did any plot exist to hand out a Nebula to a novelist who was both a Milford conferee *and* a New Wave writer, he should have been the hands-down beneficiary.

I could offer a similar analysis of the rest of the voting, but I think it unnecessary; another conspiracy theory of history has already fallen apart. To those SFWA members who may object to my washing this linen in public, and to non-members who find it simply dull, I can only reply that the giving of such awards is a highly public act, and that we owe it to the winners to dispel, if we can, any shadow that may be cast upon their laurels.

For the further record, the 1970 nominees not represented in this anthology were: *Novella:* "Dramatic Mission" by Anne McCaffrey *(Analog Magazine)*, "Probable Cause" by Charles Harness *(Orbit 4,* G. P. Putnam's Sons), "Ship of Shadows" by Fritz Leiber *(Fantasy & Science Fiction)* and "To Jorslem" by Robert Silverberg *(Galaxy Magazine); Novelet:* "The Big Flash" by Norman Spinrad *(Orbit 5)* and "Deeper Than The Darkness" by Greg Benford *(F&SF); Short story:* "Last Flight of Dr. Ain" by James Tiptree, Jr. *(Galaxy)* and "Shattered Like a Glass Goblin" by Harlan Ellison *(Orbit 4).* I omit these with apologies to all. Space is limited, and choice difficult.

And many thanks to Lloyd Biggle, Jr., and Anne McCaffrey for stalwart help with this volume, which like its four predecessors had to be assembled in one month—a task almost as difficult as figuring out how to engrave BEST NOVELET 1969 TIME CONSIDERED AS A HELIX OF SEMI-PRECIOUS STONES SAMUEL R. DELANY on a plate with about the area of an opened match folder. Please, friends, turn these thesis-titles into first lines, or you'll have to show your Nebula to friends under a reading-glass!

JAMES BLISH

HARPSDEN (HENLEY)
OXON., ENGLAND

NEBULA
AWARD
STORIES
FIVE

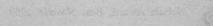

It would be easy for someone who had read no other Ellison to assume that the story which follows was written solely to shock; but Ellison is not the kind of writer who throws out Bad Words simply to shock. A little patience with its surface brutality reveals an underlying poetry, and a kind of romantic violence, more akin to the Jacobean "tragedy of blood" than to the longueurs *of naturalism. The surface will, alas, inevitably be much imitated, since no SF writer ever got away with so much cussin' before; but the close reader will see that in this particular case, the hair had to be there to be honest to the dog beneath the skin.*

A BOY AND HIS DOG

Harlan Ellison

I

I was out with Blood, my dog. It was his week for annoying me; he kept calling me Albert. He thought that was pretty damned funny. Payson Terhune: ha ha. I'd caught a couple of water rats for him, the big green and ochre ones, and someone's manicured poodle, lost off a leash in one of the downunders; he'd eaten pretty good, but he was cranky. "Come on, son of a bitch," I demanded, "find me a piece of ass." Blood just chuckled, deep in his dog-throat. "You're funny when you get horny," he said.

Maybe funny enough to kick him upside his sphincter asshole, that refugee from a dingo-heap.

"Find! I ain't kidding."

 Nebula Award, Best Novella 1969

"For shame, Albert. After all I've taught you. Not: '*I ain't* kidding.' I'm *not* kidding."

He knew I'd reached the edge of my patience. Sullenly, he started casting. He sat down on the crumbled remains of the curb, and his eyelids flickered and closed, and his hairy body tensed. After a while he settled forward on his front paws, and scraped them forward till he was lying flat, his shaggy head on the outstretched paws. The tenseness left him and he began trembling, almost the way he trembled just preparatory to scratching a flea. It went on that way for almost a quarter of an hour, and finally he rolled over and lay on his back, his naked belly toward the night sky, his front paws folded mantis-like, his hind legs extended and open. "I'm sorry," he said. "There's nothing."

I could have gotten mad and booted him, but I knew he had tried. I wasn't happy about it, I really wanted to get laid, but what could I do? "Okay," I said, with resignation, "forget it."

He kicked himself onto his side and quickly got up. "What do you want to do?" he asked.

"Not much we *can* do, is there?" I was more than a little sarcastic. He sat down again, at my feet, insolently humble.

I leaned against the melted stub of a lamppost, and thought about girls. It was painful. "We can always go to a show," I said. Blood looked around the street, at the pools of shadow lying in the weed-overgrown craters, and didn't say anything. The whelp was waiting for me to say okay, let's go. He liked movies as much as I did.

"Okay, let's go."

He got up and followed me, his tongue hanging, panting with happiness. Go ahead and laugh, you eggsucker. No popcorn for *you!*

Our Gang was a roverpak that had never been able to cut it simply foraging, so they'd opted for comfort and gone a smart way to getting it. They were movie-oriented kids, and they'd taken over the turf where the Metropole Theater was located. No one tried to bust their turf, because we all needed the movies, and as long as Our Gang had access to films, and did a better job of keeping the

16

films going, they provided a service, even for solos like me and Blood. *Especially* for solos like us.

They made me check my .45 and the Browning .22 long at the door. There was a little alcove right beside the ticket booth. I bought my tickets first; it cost me a can of Oscar Meyer Philadelphia Scrapple for me, and a tin of sardines for Blood. Then the Our Gang guards with the bren guns motioned me over to the alcove and I checked my heat. I saw water leaking from a broken pipe in the ceiling and I told the checker, a kid with big leathery warts all over his face and lips, to move my weapons where it was dry. He ignored me. "Hey, you! Mother-fuckin' toad, move my stuff over the other side . . . it goes to rust fast . . . an' it picks up any spots, man, I'll break your bones!"

He started to give me jaw about it, looked at the guards with the brens, knew if they tossed me out I'd lose my price of admission whether I went in or not, but they weren't looking for any action, probably under-strength, and gave him the nod to let it pass, to do what I said. So the toad moved my Browning to the other end of the gun rack, and pegged my .45 under it.

Blood and I went into the theater.

"I want popcorn."

"Forget it."

"Come on, Albert. Buy me popcorn."

"I'm tapped out. You can live without popcorn."

"You're just being a shit." I shrugged: sue me.

We went in. The place was jammed. I was glad the guards hadn't tried to take anything but guns. My spike and knife felt reassuring, lying-up in their oiled sheaths at the back of my neck. Blood found two together, and we moved into the row, stepping on feet. Someone cursed and I ignored him. A Doberman growled. Blood's fur stirred, but he let it pass. There was always *some* hardcase on the muscle, even in neutral ground like the Metropole.

(I heard once about a get-it-on they'd had at the old Loew's Granada, on the South Side. Wound up with ten or twelve rovers and their mutts dead, the theater burned down and a couple of good Cagney films lost in the fire. After that was when the roverpaks had got up the agreement that movie houses were sanctuaries. It was better now, but there was always somebody too messed in the mind to come soft.)

It was a triple feature. "Raw Deal" with Dennis O'Keefe, Claire Trevor, Raymond Burr and Marsha Hunt was the oldest of the three. It'd been made in 1948, seventy-six years ago, god only knows how the damn thing'd hung together all that time; it slipped sprockets and they had to stop the movie all the time to re-thread it. But it was a good movie. About this solo who'd been japped by his roverpak and was out to get revenge. Gangsters, mobs, a lot of punching and fighting. Real good.

The middle flick was a thing made during the Third War, in '07, two years before I was even born, thing called "Smell of a Chink". It was mostly gut-spilling and some nice hand-to-hand. Beautiful scene of skirmisher greyhounds equipped with napalm throwers, jellyburning a Chink town. Blood dug it, even though we'd seen this flick before. He had some kind of phony shuck going that these were ancestors of his, and *he* knew and I knew he was making it up.

"Wanna burn a baby, hero?" I whispered to him. He got the barb and just shifted in his seat, didn't say a thing, kept looking pleased as the dogs worked their way through the town. I was bored stiff.

I was waiting for the main feature.

Finally it came on. It was a beauty, a beaver flick made in the late 1970's. It was called "Big Black Leather Splits". Started right out very good. These two blondes in black leather corsets and boots laced all the way up to their crotches, with whips and masks, got this skinny guy down and one of the chicks sat on his face while the other one went down on him. It got really hairy after that.

All around me there were solos playing with themselves. I was about to jog it a little myself when Blood leaned across and said, real soft, the way he does when he's onto something unusually smelly, "There's a chick in here."

"You're nuts," I said.

"I tell you I smell her. She's in here, man."

Without being conspicuous, I looked around. Almost every seat in the theater was taken with solos or their dogs. If a chick had slipped in there'd have been a riot. She'd have been ripped to pieces before any single guy could have gotten into her. "Where?" I asked, softly. All around me, the solos were beating-off, moaning as the blondes took off their masks and one of them worked the skinny guy with a big wooden ram strapped around her hips.

"Give me a minute," Blood said. He was really concentrating. His body was tense as a wire. His eyes were closed, his muzzle quivering. I let him work.

It was possible. Just maybe possible. I knew that they made really dumb flicks in the downunders, the kind of crap they'd made back in the 1930's and '40's, real clean stuff with even married people sleeping in twin beds. Myrna Loy and George Brent kind of flicks. And I knew that once in a while a chick from one of the really strict middle-class downunders would cumup, to see what a hairy flick was like. I'd heard about it, but it'd never happened in any theater *I'd* ever been in.

And the chances of it happening in the Metropole, particularly, were slim. There was a lot of twisty trade came to the Metropole. Now, understand, I'm not specially prejudiced against guys corning one another . . . hell, I can understand it. There just aren't enough chicks anywhere. But I can't cut the jockey-and-boxer scene because it gets some weak little boxer hanging on you, getting jealous, you have to hunt for him and all he thinks he has to do is bare his ass to get all the work done for him. It's as bad as having a chick dragging along behind. Made for a lot of bad blood and fights in the bigger roverpaks, too. So I just never swung that way. Well, not *never*, but not for a long time.

So with all the twisties in the Metropole, I didn't think a chick would chance it. Be a toss-up who'd tear her apart first: the boxers or the straights.

And if she *was* here, why couldn't any of the other dogs smell her . . . ?

"Third row in front of us," Blood said. "Aisle seat. Dressed like a solo."

"How's come *you* can whiff her and no other dog's caught her?"

"You forget who I am, Albert."

"I don't forget, I just don't believe it."

Actually, bottom-line, I guess I *did* believe it. When you'd been as dumb as I'd been and a dog like Blood's taught me so much, a guy came to believe *everything* he said. You don't argue with your teacher.

Not when he's taught you how to read and write and add and subtract and everything else they used to know that meant you were smart (but doesn't mean much of anything now, except it's good to know it, I guess).

(The reading's a pretty good thing. It comes in handy when you can find some canned goods someplace, like in a bombed-out supermarket; makes it easier to pick out stuff you like when the pictures are gone off the labels. Couple of times the reading stopped me from taking canned beets. Shit, I *hate* beets!)

So I guess I *did* believe why he could whiff a maybe chick in there, and no other mutt could. He'd told me all about *that* a million times. It was his favorite story. History he called it. Christ, I'm not *that* dumb! I knew what history was. That was all the stuff that happened before now.

But I liked hearing history straight from Blood, instead of him making me read one of those crummy books he was always dragging in. And *that* particular history was all about him, so he laid it on me over and over till I knew it by heart . . . no, the word was *rote*. Not *wrote,* like writing, that was something else. I knew it by rote, like it means you got it word-for-word.

And when a mutt teaches you everything you know, and he tells you something rote, I guess finally you *do* believe it. Except I'd never let that leg-lifter know it.

II

What he'd told me rote was:

Over fifty years ago, in Los Angeles, before the Third War even got going completely, there was a man named Buesing who lived in Cerritos. He raised dogs as watchmen and sentries and attackers. Dobermans, Danes, Schnauzers and Japanese Akitas. He had one 4-year-old German shepherd bitch named Ginger. She worked for the Los Angeles Police Department's narcotics division. She could smell out marijuana. No matter how well it was hidden. They ran a test on her: there were 25,000 boxes in an auto parts warehouse. Five of them had been planted with marijuana that had been sealed in cellophane, wrapped in tin foil and heavy brown paper, and finally hidden in three separate sealed cartons. Within seven minutes Ginger found all five packages. At the same time that Ginger was working, ninety-two miles further north, in Santa Barbara, cetologists had drawn and amplified dolphin spinal fluid and injected it into Chacma baboons and dogs. Altering surgery and grafting had been done. The first successful product of this cetacean experimentation had been a 2-year-old male Puli named Ahbhu, who had communicated sense-impressions telepathically. Cross-breeding and continued experimentation had produced the first skirmisher dogs, just in time for the Third War. Telepathic over short distances, easily trained, able to track gasoline or troops or poison gas or radiation when linked with their human controllers, they had become the shock commandos of a new kind of war. The selective traits had bred true. Dobermans, Greyhounds, Akitas, Pulis and Schnauzers had become steadily more telepathic.

Ginger and Ahbhu had been Blood's ancestors.

He had told me so, a thousand times. Had told me the story just that way, in just those words, a thousand times, as it had been told to him. I'd never believed him till now.

Maybe the little bastard *was* special.

I checked out the solo scrunched down in the aisle seat three rows ahead of me. I couldn't tell a damned thing. The solo had his (her?) cap pulled way down, fleece jacket pulled way up.

"Are you sure?"

"As sure as I can be. It's a girl."

"If it is, she's playing with herself just like a guy." Blood snickered. "Surprise," he said sarcastically.

The mystery solo sat through "Raw Deal" again. It made sense, if that was a girl. Most of the solos and all of the members of roverpaks left after the beaver flick. The theater didn't fill up much more, it gave the streets time to empty, he/she could make his/her way back to wherever he/she had come from. I sat through "Raw Deal" again myself. Blood went to sleep.

When the mystery solo got up, I gave him/her time to get weapons if any'd been checked, and start away. Then

I pulled Blood's big shaggy ear and said, "Let's do it." He slouched after me, up the aisle.

I got my guns and checked the street. Empty.

"Okay, nose," I said, "where'd he go?"

"Her. To the right."

I started off, loading the Browning from my bandolier. I still didn't see anyone moving among the bombed-out shells of the buildings. This section of the city was crummy, really bad shape. But then, with Our Gang running the Metropole, they didn't have to repair anything else to get their livelihood. It was ironic; the Dragons had to keep an entire power plant going to get tribute from the other roverpaks, Ted's Bunch had to mind the reservoir, the Bastinados worked like field-hands in the marijuana gardens, the Barbados Blacks lost a couple of dozen members every year cleaning out the radiation pits all over the city; and Our Gang only had to run that movie house.

Whoever their leader had been, however many years ago it had been that the roverpaks had started forming out of foraging solos, I had to give it to him: he'd been a flinty sharp mother. He knew what services to deal in.

"She turned off here," Blood said.

I followed him as he began loping, toward the edge of the city and the bluish-green radiation that still flickered from the hills. I knew he was right, then. The only thing out here was the access dropshaft to the downunder. It was a girl, all right.

The cheeks of my ass tightened as I thought about it. I was going to get laid. It had been almost a month, since Blood had whiffled that solo chick in the basement of the Market Basket. She'd been filthy, and I'd gotten the crabs from her, but she'd been a woman, all right, and once I'd tied her down and clubbed her a couple of times she'd been pretty good. She'd liked it, too, even if she did spit on me and tell me she'd kill me if she ever got loose. I left her tied up, just to be sure. She wasn't there when I went back to look, week before last.

"Watch out," Blood said, dodging around a crater almost invisible against the surrounding shadows. Something stirred in the crater.

Trekking across the nomansland I realized why it was that all but a handful of solos or members of roverpaks were guys. The War had killed off most of the girls, and that was the way it always was in wars . . . at least that's what Blood told me. The things getting born were seldom male *or* female, and had to be smashed against a wall as soon as they were pulled out of the mother.

The few chicks who hadn't gone downunder with the middle-classers were hard, solitary bitches like the one in the Market Basket; tough and stringy and just as likely to cut off your meat with a razor blade once they let you get in. Scuffling for a piece of ass had gotten harder and harder, the older I'd gotten.

But every once in a while a chick got tired of being roverpak property, or a raid was got-up by five or six roverpaks and some unsuspecting downunder was taken, or—like this time, yeah—some middle-class chick from a downunder got hot pants to find out what a beaver flick looked like, and cumup.

I was going to get laid. Oh boy, I couldn't wait!

III

Out here it was nothing but empty corpses of blasted buildings. One entire block had been stomped flat, like a steel press had come down from Heaven and given one solid wham! and everything was powder under it. The chick was scared and skittish, I could see that. She moved erratically, looking back over her shoulder and to either side. She knew she was in dangerous country. Man, if she'd only known *how* dangerous.

There was one building standing all alone at the end of the smashflat block, like it had been missed and chance let it stay. She ducked inside, and a minute later I saw a bobbing light. Flashlight? Maybe.

Blood and I crossed the street and came up into the blackness surrounding the building. It was what was left of a YMCA.

That meant "Young Men's Christian Association." Blood taught me to read.

So what the hell was a young men's christian association. Sometimes being able to read makes more questions than if you were stupid.

I didn't want her getting out; inside there was as good a place to screw her as any, so I put Blood on guard right beside the steps leading up into the shell, and I went around the back. All the doors and windows had been blown out, of course. It wasn't no big trick getting in. I pulled myself up to the ledge of a window, and dropped down inside. Dark inside. No noise, except the sound of her, moving around on the other side of the old YMCA. I didn't know if she was heeled or not, and I wasn't about to take any chances. I bowslung the Browning and took out the .45 automatic. I didn't have to snap back the action—there was always a slug in the chamber.

I started moving carefully through the room. It was a locker room of some kind. There was glass and debris all over the floor, and one entire row of metal lockers had the paint blistered off their surfaces; the flash blast had caught them through the windows, a lot of years ago. My sneakers didn't make a sound coming through the room.

The door was hanging on one hinge, and I stepped over —through the inverted triangle. I was in the swimming pool area. The big pool was empty, with tiles buckled down at the shallow end. It stunk bad in there; no wonder, there were dead guys, or what was left of them, along one wall. Some lousy cleaner-up had stacked them, but hadn't buried them. I pulled my bandana up around my nose and mouth, and kept moving.

Out the other side of the pool place, and through a little passage with popped light bulbs in the ceiling. I didn't have any trouble seeing. There was moonlight coming through busted windows and a chunk was out of the ceiling. I could hear her real plain now, just on the other side of the door at the end of the passage. I hung close to the wall, and stepped down to the door. It was open a crack, but blocked by a fall of lath and plaster from the wall. It would make noise when I went to pull it open, that was for certain. I had to wait for the right moment.

Flattened against the wall, I checked out what she was doing in there. It was a gymnasium, big one, with climbing ropes hanging down from the ceiling. She had a big square eight-cell flashlight sitting up on the croup of a vaulting horse. There were parallel bars and a horizontal bar about eight feet high, the high-tempered steel all rusty now. There were swinging rings and a trampoline and a big wooden balancing beam. Over to one side there were wallbars and balancing benches, horizontal and oblique ladders, and a couple of stacks of vaulting boxes. I made a note to remember this joint. It was better for working-out than the jerry-rigged gym I'd set up in an old auto wrecking yard. A guy has to keep in shape, if he's going to be a solo.

She was out of her disguise. Standing there in the skin, shivering. Yeah, it was chilly, and I could see a pattern of chicken-skin all over her. She was maybe five six or seven, with nice tits and kind of skinny legs. She was brushing out her hair. It hung way down the back. The flashlight didn't make it clear enough to tell if she had red hair or chestnut, but it wasn't blonde, which was good, and that was because I dug redheads. She had nice tits, though. I couldn't see her face, the hair was hanging down all smooth and wavy and cut off her profile.

The crap she'd been wearing was laying around on the floor, and what she was going to put on was up on the vaulting horse. She was standing in little shoes with a kind of funny heel on them.

I couldn't move. I suddenly realized I couldn't move. She was nice, really nice. I was getting as big a kick out of just standing there and seeing the way her waist fell inward and her hips fell outward, the way the muscles at the side of her tits pulled up when she reached to the top of her head to brush all that hair down. It was really weird, the kick I was getting out of standing and just staring at a chick do that. Kind of very, well, woman stuff. I liked it a lot.

I'd never ever stopped and just looked at a chick like that. All the ones I'd ever seen had been scumbags that Blood had smelled out for me, and I'd snatchn'grabbed them. Or the big chicks in the beaver flicks. Not like this one, kind of soft and very smooth, even with the goose bumps. I could of watched her all night.

She put down the brush, and reached over and took a pair of panties off the pile of clothes, and wriggled into them. Then she got her bra and put it on. I never knew the way chicks did it. She put it on backwards, around her waist, and it had a hook on it. Then she slid it around till the cups were in front, and kind of pulled it up under and scooped herself into it, first one, then the other; then she pulled the straps over her shoulder. She reached for her dress, and I nudged some of the lath and plaster aside, and grabbed the door to give it a yank.

She had the dress up over her head, and her arms up inside the material, and when she stuck her head in, and was all tangled there for a second, I yanked the door and there was a crash as chunks of wood and plaster fell out of the way, and a heavy scraping, and I jumped inside and was on her before she could get out of her dress.

She started to scream, and I pulled the dress off her with a ripping sound, and it all happened for her before she knew what that crash and scrape was all about.

Her face was wild. Just wild. Big eyes: I couldn't tell what color they were because they were in shadow. Real fine features, a wide mouth, little nose, cheekbones just like mine, real high and prominent and a dimple in her right cheek. She stared at me really scared.

And then . . . and this is really weird . . . I felt like I should *say* something to her. I don't know what. Just something. It made me uncomfortable, to see her scared, but what the hell could I do about *that*. I mean, I was going to rape her, after all, and I couldn't very well tell her not to be shrinky about it. She was the one cumup, after all. But even so, I wanted to say hey, don't be scared, I just want to lay you. (That never happened before. I never wanted to *say* anything to a chick, just get in, and that was that.)

But it passed, and I put my leg behind hers and tripped her back, and she went down in a pile. I leveled the .45 at her, and her mouth kind of opened in a little o shape. "Now I'm gonna go over there and get one of them wrestling mats, so it'll be better, comfortable, uh-huh? You make a move off that floor and I shoot a leg out from under you, and you'll get screwed just the same, except you'll be without a leg." I waited for her to let me know she was onto what I was saying and she finally nodded real slow, so I kept the automatic on her, and went over to the big dusty stack of mats, and pulled one off.

I dragged it over to her, and flipped it so the cleaner side was up, and used the muzzle of the .45 to maneuver her onto it. She just sat there on the mat, with her hands behind her, and her knees bent, and stared at me.

I unzipped my pants and started pulling them down off one side, when I caught her looking at me real funny. I stopped with the jeans. "What're *you* lookin' at?"

26

I was mad. I didn't know why I was mad, but I was.

"What's your name?" she asked. Her voice was very soft, and kind of furry, like it came up through her throat that was all lined with fur or something.

She kept looking at me, waiting for me to answer.

"Vic," I said. She looked like she was waiting for more. "Vic what?"

I didn't know what she meant for a minute, then I did. "Vic. Just Vic. That's all."

"Well, what're your mother and father's names?"

Then I started laughing, and working my jeans down again. "Boy, are you a dumb bitch," I said, and laughed some more. She looked hurt. It made me mad again. "Stop lookin' like that, or I'll bust out your teeth!"

She folded her hands in her lap.

I got the pants down around my ankles. They wouldn't come off over the sneakers. I had to balance on one foot and scuff the sneaker off the other foot. It was tricky, keeping the .45 on her and getting the sneaker off at the same time. But I did it.

I was standing there buck-naked from the waist down and she had sat forward a little, her legs crossed, hands still in her lap. "Get that stuff off," I said.

She didn't move for a second, and I thought she was going to give me trouble. But then she reached around behind and undid the bra. Then she tipped back and slipped the panties off her ass.

Suddenly, she didn't look scared any more. She was watching me very close and I could see her eyes were blue now. Now this is the really weird thing . . .

I couldn't do it. I mean, not exactly. I mean, I *wanted* to fuck her, see, but she was all soft and pretty and she kept *looking* at me, and no solo I ever met would believe me, but I heard myself *talking* to her, still standing there like some kind of wetbrain, one sneaker off and jeans down around my ankle. "What's *your* name?"

"Quilla June Holmes."

"That's a weird name."

"My mother says it's not that uncommon, back in Oklahoma."

"That where your folks come from?"

She nodded. "Before the Third War."

"They must be pretty old by now."

27

"They are, but they're okay. I guess."

We were just frozen there, talking to each other. I could tell she was cold, because she was shivering. "Well," I said, sort of getting ready to drop down beside her, "I guess we better—"

Damn it! That damned Blood! Right at that moment he came dashing in from outside. Came skidding through the lath, and plaster, raising dust, slid along on his ass till he got to us. *"Now* what?" I demanded.

"Who're you talking to?" the girl asked.

"Him. Blood."

"The dog!?!"

Blood stared at her and then ignored her. He started to say something, but the girl interrupted him, "Then it's true what they say . . . you can all talk to animals . . ."

"You going to listen to her all night, or do you want to hear why I came in?"

"Okay, why're you here?"

"You're in trouble, Albert."

"Come *on,* forget the mickeymouse. What's up?"

Blood twisted his head toward the front door of the YMCA. "Roverpak. Got the building surrounded. I make it fifteen or twenty, maybe more."

"How the hell'd they know we was here?"

Blood looked chagrined. He dropped his head.

"Well?"

"Some other mutt must've smelled her in the theater?"

"Great."

"Now what?"

"Now we stand 'em off, that's what. You got any better suggestions?"

"Just one."

I waited. He grinned.

"Pull your pants up."

IV

The girl, this Quilla June, was pretty safe. I made her a kind of shelter out of wrestling mats, maybe a dozen of them. She wouldn't get hit by a stray bullet, and if they didn't go right for her, they wouldn't find her. I climbed one of the ropes hanging down from the girders and laid

28

out up there with the Browning and a couple of handfuls of reloads. I wished to God I'd had an automatic, a bren or a Thompson. I checked the .45, made sure it was full, with one in the chamber, and set the extra clips down on the girder. I had a clear line-of-fire all around the gym.

Blood was lying in shadow right near the front door. He'd suggested I try and pick off any dog with the rover-pak first, if I could. That would allow him to operate freely.

That was the least of my worries.

I'd wanted to hole up in another room, one with only a single entrance, but I had no way of knowing if the rovers were already in the building, so I did the best I could with what I had.

Everything was quiet. Even that Quilla June. It'd taken me valuable minutes to convince her she'd damned well better hole up and not make any noise, she was better off with me than with twenty of *them.* "If you ever wanna see your mommy and daddy again," I warned her. After that she didn't give me no trouble, packing her in with mats.

Quiet.

Then I heard two things, both at the same time. From back in the swimming pool I heard boots crunching plaster. Very soft. And from one side of the front door I heard a tinkle of metal striking wood. So they were going to try a yoke. Well, I was ready.

Quiet again.

I sighted the Browning on the door to the pool room. It was still open from when I'd come through. Figure him at maybe five-ten, and drop the sights a foot and a half, and I'd catch him in the chest. I'd learned long ago you don't try for the head. Go for the widest part of the body: the chest and stomach. The trunk.

Suddenly, outside, I heard a dog bark, and part of the darkness near the front door detached itself and moved inside the gym. Directly opposite Blood. I didn't move the Browning.

The rover at the front door moved a step along the wall, away from Blood. Then he cocked back his arm and threw something—a rock, a piece of metal, some-thing—across the room, to draw fire. I didn't move the Browning.

When the thing he'd thrown hit the floor, two rovers jumped out of the swimming pool door, one on either side of it, rifles down, ready to spray. Before they could open up, I'd squeezed off the first shot, tracked across and put a second shot into the other one. They both went down. Dead hits, right in the heart. Bang, they were down, neither one moved.

The mother by the door turned to split, and Blood was on him. Just like that, out of the darkness, riiiip!

Blood leaped, right over the crossbar of the guy's rifle held at ready, and sank his fangs into the rover's throat. The guy screamed, and Blood dropped, carrying a piece of the guy with him. The guy was making awful bubbling sounds and went down on one knee. I put a slug into his head, and he fell forward.

It went quiet again.

Not bad. Not bad atall atall. Three takeouts and they still didn't know our positions. Blood had fallen back into the murk by the entrance. He didn't say a thing, but I knew he was thinking: maybe that was three out of seventeen, or three out of twenty, or twenty-two. No way of knowing; we could be face-off in here for a week and never know if we'd gotten them all, or some, or none. They could go and get poured full again, and I'd find myself run out of slugs and no food and that girl, that Quilla June, crying and making me divide my attention, and daylight—and they'd be still laying out there, waiting till we got hungry enough to do something dumb, or till we ran out of slugs, and then they'd cloud up and rain all over us.

A rover came dashing straight through the front door at top speed, took a leap, hit on his shoulders, rolled, came up going in a different direction and snapped off three rounds into different corners of the room before I could track him with the Browning. By that time he was close enough under me where I didn't have to waste a .22 slug. I picked up the .45 without a sound and blew the back off his head. Slug went in neat, came out and took most of his hair with it. He fell right down.

"Blood! The rifle!"

Came out of the shadows, grabbed it up in his mouth and dragged it over to the pile of wrestling mats in the far corner. I saw an arm poke out from the mass of mats, and a hand grabbed the rifle, dragged it inside. Well, it was at least safe there, till I needed it. Brave little bastard: he scuttled over to the dead rover and started worrying the ammo bandolier off his body. It took him a while; he could have been picked off from the doorway or outside one of the windows, but he did it. Brave little bastard. I had to remember to get him something good to eat, when we got out of this. I smiled, up there in the darkness: *if* we get out of this, I wouldn't have to worry about getting him something tender. It was lying all over the floor of that gymnasium.

Just as Blood was dragging the bandolier back into the shadows, two of them tried it with their dogs. They came through a ground floor window, one after another, hitting and rolling and going in opposite directions, as the dogs —a mother-ugly Akita, big as a house, and a Doberman bitch the color of a turd—shot through the front door and split in the unoccupied two directions. I caught one of the dogs, the Akita, with the .45 and it went down thrashing. The Doberman was all over Blood.

But firing, I'd given away my position. One of the rovers fired from the hip and .30-06 soft-nosed slugs spanged off the girders around me. I dropped the automatic, and it started to slip off the girder as I reached for the Browning. I made a grab for the .45 and that was the only thing saved me. I fell forward to clutch at it, it slipped away and hit the gym floor with a crash, and the rover fired at where I'd been. But I was flat on the girder, arm dangling, and the crash startled him. He fired at the sound, and right at that instant I heard another shot, from a Winchester, and the other rover, who'd made it safe into the shadows, fell forward holding a big pumping hole in his chest. That Quilla June had shot him, from behind the mats.

I didn't even have time to figure out what the fuck was happening . . . Blood was rolling around with the Doberman and the sounds they were making were awful . . . the rover with the .30-06 chipped off another shot and hit the muzzle of the Browning, protruding over the side of the girder, and wham it was gone, falling down. I was naked up there without clout, and the sonobitch was hanging back in shadow waiting for me.

Another shot from the Winchester, and the rover fired

right into the mats. She ducked back behind, and I knew I couldn't count on her for anything more. But I didn't need it; in that second, while he was focused on her, I grabbed the climbing rope, flipped myself over the girder, and howling like a burnpit-screamer, went sliding down, feeling the rope cutting my palms. I got down far enough to swing, and kicked off. I swung back and forth, whipping my body three different ways each time, swinging out and over, way over, each time. The sonofabitch kept firing, trying to track a trajectory, but I kept spinning out of his line of fire. Then he was empty, and I kicked back as hard as I could, and came zooming in toward his corner of shadows, and let loose all at once and went ass-over-end into the corner, and there he was, and I went right into him and he spanged off the wall, and I was on top of him, digging my thumbs into his eye-sockets. He was screaming and the dogs were screaming and that girl was screaming, and I pounded the mother-fucker's head against the floor till he stopped moving, then I grabbed up the empty .30-06 and whipped his head till I knew he wasn't gonna give me no more aggravation.

Then I found the .45 and shot the Doberman.

Blood got up and shook himself off. He was cut up bad. "Thanks," he mumbled, and went over and lay down in the shadows to lick himself off.

I went and found that Quilla June, and she was crying. About all the guys we'd killed. Mostly about the one *she'd* killed. I couldn't get her to stop bawling, so I cracked her across the face, and told her she'd saved my life, and that helped some.

Blood came dragassing over. "How're we going to get out of this, Albert?"

"Let me think."

I thought, and knew it was hopeless. No matter how many we got, there'd be more. And it was a matter of *macho* now. Their honor.

"How about a fire?" Blood suggested.

"Get away while it's burning?" I shook my head. "They'll have the place staked-out all around. No good."

"What if we don't leave? What if we burn up with it?"

I looked at him. Brave . . . and smart as hell.

V

We gathered all the lumber and mats and scaling ladders and vaulting boxes and benches and anything else that would burn, and piled the garbage against a wooden divider at one end of the gym. Quilla June found a can of kerosene in a storeroom, and we set fire to the whole damn pile. Then we followed Blood to the place he'd found for us. The boiler room way down under the YMCA. We all climbed into the empty boiler, and dogged down the door, leaving a release vent open for air. We had one mat in there with us, and all the ammo we could carry, and the extra rifles and sidearms the rovers'd had on them.

"Can you catch anything?" I asked Blood.

"A little. Not much. I'm reading one guy. The building's burning good."

"You be able to tell when they split?"

"Maybe. *If* they split."

I settled back. Quilla June was shaking from all that had happened. "Just take it easy," I told her. "By morning the place'll be down around our ears and they'll go through the rubble and find a lot of dead meat and maybe they won't look too hard for a chick's body. And everything'll be all right . . . if we don't get choked off in here."

She smiled, very thin, and tried to look brave. She was okay, that one. She closed her eyes and settled back on the mat and tried to sleep. I was beat. I closed my eyes, too.

"Can you handle it?" I asked Blood.

"I suppose. You better sleep."

I nodded, eyes still closed, and fell on my side. I was out before I could think about it.

When I came back, I found the girl, that Quilla June, snuggled up under my armpit, her arm around my waist, dead asleep. I could hardly breathe. It was like a furnace; hell, it *was* a furnace. I reached out a hand and the wall of the boiler was so damned hot I couldn't touch it. Blood was up on the mattress with us. That mat had been the only thing'd kept us from being singed good. He was asleep, head buried in his paws. She was asleep, still naked.

I put a hand on her tit. It was warm, She stirred and cuddled into me closer. I got a hard on.

Managed to get my pants off, and rolled on top of her. She woke up fast when she felt me pry her legs apart, but it was too late by then. "Don't ... *stop* ... what are you doing ... no, don't ..."

But she was half-asleep, and weak, and I don't think she really wanted to fight me anyhow.

She cried when I broke her, of course, but after that it was okay. There was blood all over the wrestling mat. And Blood just kept sleeping.

It was really different. Usually, when I'd get Blood to track something down for me, it'd be grab it and punch it and get away fast before something bad could happen. But when she came, she rose up off the mat, and hugged me around the back so hard I thought she'd crack my ribs, and then she settled back down slow slow slow, like I do when I'm doing leg-lifts in the makeshift gym I rigged in the auto wrecking yard. And her eyes were closed, and she was relaxed looking. And happy. I could tell.

We did it a lot of times, and after a while it was her idea but I didn't say no. And then we lay out side-by-side and talked.

She asked me about how it was with Blood, and I told her how the skirmisher dogs had gotten telepathic, and how they'd lost the ability to hunt food for themselves, so the solos and roverpaks had to do it for them, and how dogs like Blood were good at finding chicks for solos like me. She didn't say anything to that.

I asked her about what it was like where she lived, in one of the downunders.

"It's nice. But it's always very quiet. Everyone is very polite to everyone else. It's just a small town."

"Which one you live in?"

"Topeka. It's real close to here."

"Yeah, I know. The access dropshaft is only about half a mile from here. I went out there once, to take a look around."

"Have you ever been in a downunder?"

"No. But I don't guess I want to be, either."

"Why? It's very nice. You'd like it."

"Shit."

"That's very crude."

"*I'm* very crude."

"Not all the time."

I was getting mad. "Listen, you ass, what's the matter with you? I grabbed you and pushed you around, I raped you half a dozen times, so what's so good about me, huh? What's the matter with you, don't you even have enough smarts to know when somebody's—"

She was smiling at me. "I didn't mind. I liked doing it. Want to do it again?"

I was really shocked. I moved away from her. "What the hell is wrong with you? Don't you know that a chick from a downunder like you can be really mauled by solos? Don't you know chicks get warnings from their parents in the downunders, 'Don't cumup, you'll get snagged by them dirty, hairy, slobbering solos!' Don't you know that?"

She put her hand on my leg and started moving it up, the fingertips just brushing my thigh. I got another hard on. "My parents never said that about solos," she said. Then she pulled me over her again, and kissed me and I couldn't stop from getting in her again.

God, it just went on like that for hours. After a while Blood turned around and said, "I'm not going to keep pretending I'm asleep. I'm hungry. And I'm hurt."

I tossed her off me—she was on top by this time—and examined him. The Doberman had taken a good chunk out of his right ear, and there was a rip right down his muzzle, and blood-matted fur on one side. He was a mess. "Jesus, you're a mess," I said.

"You're no fucking rose garden yourself, Albert!" he snapped. I pulled my hand back.

"Can we get out of here?" I asked him.

He cast around, and then shook his head. "I can't get any readings. Must be a pile of rubble on top of this boiler. I'll have to go out and scout."

We kicked that around for a while, and finally decided if the building was razed, and had cooled a little, the roverpak would have gone through the ashes by now. The fact that they hadn't tried the boiler indicated that we were probably buried pretty good. Either that, or the building was still smoldering overhead. In which case, they'd still be out there, waiting to sift the remains.

"Think you can handle it, the condition you're in?"

"I guess I'll *have* to, won't I?" Blood said. He was really surly. "I mean, what with you busy fucking your brains out, there won't be much left for staying alive, will there?"

I sensed real trouble with him. He didn't like Quilla June. I moved around him and undogged the boiler hatch. It wouldn't open. So I braced my back against the side, and jacked my legs up, and gave it a slow, steady shove.

Whatever had fallen against it from outside, resisted for a minute, then started to give, then tumbled away with a crash. I pushed the door open all the way, and looked out. The upper floors had fallen in on the basement, but by the time they'd given, they'd been mostly cinder and lightweight rubble. Everything was smoking out there. I could see daylight through the smoke.

I slipped out, burning my hands on the outside lip of the hatch. Blood followed. He started to pick his way through the debris. I could see that the boiler had been almost completely covered by the gunk that had dropped from above. Chances were good the roverpak had taken a fast look, figured we'd been fried, and moved on. But I wanted Blood to run a recon, anyway. He started off, but I called him back. He came.

"What is it?"

I looked down at him. "I'll tell you what it is, man. You're acting very shitty."

"Sue me."

"Goddamit, dog, what's got your ass up?"

"Her. That nit chick you've got in there."

"So what? Big deal . . . I've had chicks before."

"Yeah, but never any that hung on like this one. I warn you, Albert, she's going to make trouble."

"Don't be dumb!" He didn't reply. Just looked at me with anger, and then scampered off to check out the scene. I crawled back inside and dogged the hatch. She wanted to make it again. I said I didn't want to; Blood had brought me down. I was bugged. And I didn't know which one to be pissed off at.

But God she was pretty.

She kind of pouted, and settled back with her arms

wrapped around her. "Tell me some more about the down-under," I said.

At first she was cranky, wouldn't say much, but after a while she opened up and started talking freely. I was learning a lot. I figured I could use it some time, maybe.

There were only a couple of hundred downunders in what was left of the United States and Canada. They'd been sunk on the sites of wells or mines or other kinds of deep holes. Some of them, out in the west, were in natural cave formations. They went way down, maybe two to five miles. They were like big caissons, stood on end. And the people who'd settled them were squares of the worst kind. Southern Baptists, Fundamentalists, lawanorder goofs, real middleclass squares with no taste for the wild life. And they'd gone back to a kind of life that hadn't existed for a hundred and fifty years. They'd gotten the last of the scientists to do the work, invent the how and why, and then they'd run them out. They didn't want any progress, they didn't want any dissent, they didn't want anything that would make waves. They'd had enough of that. The best time in the world had been just before the First War, and they figured if they could keep it like that, they could live quiet and survive. Shit! I'd go nuts in one of the downunders.

Quilla June smiled, and snuggled up again, and this time I didn't turn her off. She started touching me again, down there and all over, and then she said, "Vic?"

"Uh-huh."

"Have you ever been in love?"

"What?"

"In love? Have you ever been in love with a girl?"

"Well, I damn well guess I haven't!"

"Do you know what love is?"

"Sure. I guess I do."

"But if you've never been in love . . . ?"

"Don't be dumb. I mean, I've never had a bullet in the head, and I know I wouldn't like it."

"You don't know what love is, I'll bet."

"Well, if it means living in a downunder, I guess I just don't wanna find out." We didn't go on with the conversation much after that. She pulled me down and we did it again. And when it was over, I heard Blood scratching in

37

the boiler. I opened the hatch and he was standing out there. "All clear," he said.

"You sure?"

"Yeah, yeah, I'm sure. Put your pants on," he said it with a sneer in the tone, "and come on out here. We have to talk some stuff."

I looked at him, and he wasn't kidding. I got my jeans and sneakers on, and climbed down out of the boiler.

He trotted ahead of me, away from the boiler, over some blacksoot beams, and outside the gym. It was down. Looked like a rotted stump tooth.

"Now what's lumbering you?" I asked him.

He scampered up on a chunk of concrete till he was almost noselevel with me.

"You're going dumb on me, Vic."

I knew he was serious. No Albert shit, straight Vic. "How so?"

"Last night, man. We could have cut out of there and left her for them. *That* would've been smart."

"I wanted her."

"Yeah, I know. That's what I'm talking about. It's to-day now, not last night. You've had her about half a hundred times. Why're we hanging around?"

"I want some more."

Then he got angry. "Yeah, well, listen, chum . . . *I* want a few things myself. I want something to eat, and I want to get rid of this pain in my side, and I want away from this turf. Maybe they *don't* give up this easy."

"Take it easy. We can handle all that. Don't mean she can't go with us."

"*Doesn't* mean," he corrected me. "And so *that's* the new story. Now we travel three, is that right?"

I was getting *tres* uptight myself. "You're starting to sound like a poodle!"

"And you're starting to sound like a boxer."

I hauled back to crack him one. He didn't move. I dropped the hand. I'd never hit Blood. I didn't want to start now.

"Sorry," he said, softly.

"That's okay."

But we weren't looking at each other.

"Vic, man, you've got responsibility to me, you know."

"You don't have to tell me that."

"Well, I guess maybe I do. Maybe I have to remind you of some stuff. Like the time that burnpit-screamer came up out of the street and made a grab for you."

I shuddered. The motherfucker'd been green. Righteous stone green, glowing like fungus. My gut heaved, just thinking.

"And I went for him, right?"

I nodded. Right, mutt, right.

"And I could have been burned bad, and died, and that would've been all of it for me, right or wrong, isn't that true?" I nodded again. I was getting pissed off proper. I didn't like being made to feel guilty. It was a fifty-fifty with Blood and me. He knew that. "But I did it, right?" I remembered the way that green thing had screamed. Christ, it was like ooze and eyelashes.

"Okay, okay, don't hanger me."

"*Harangue,* not hanger."

"Well WHATEVER!" I shouted. "Just knock off the crap, or we can forget the whole fucking arrangement!"

Then Blood blew. "Well maybe we *should,* you simple dumb *putz!*"

"What's a *putz,* you little turd . . . is that something bad . . . yeah, it must be . . . you watch your fucking mouth, son of a bitch, I'll kick your ass!"

We sat there and didn't talk for fifteen minutes. Neither one of us knew which way to go.

Finally, I backed off a little. I talked soft and I talked slow. I was about up to here with him, but told him I was going to do right by him, like I always had, and he threatened me, saying I'd damned well better because there were a couple of very hip solos making it around the city, and they'd be delighted to have a sharp tail-scent like him. I told him I didn't like being threatened, and he'd better watch his fucking step or I'd break his leg. He got furious and stalked off. I said screw you and went back to the boiler to take it out on that Quilla June again.

But when I stuck my head inside the boiler, she was waiting, with a pistol one of the dead rovers had supplied. She hit me good and solid over the right eye with it, and I fell straight forward across the hatch, and was out cold.

VI

"I told you she was no good." He watched me as I swabbed out the cut with disinfectant from my kit, and painted the tear with iodine. He smirked when I flinched.

I put away the stuff, and rummaged around in the boiler, gathering up all the spare ammo I could carry, and ditching the Browning in favor of the heavier .30-06. Then I found something that must've slipped out of her clothes.

It was a little metal plate, about 3½ inches long and an inch and a half high. It had a whole string of numbers on it, and there were holes in it, in random patterns. "What's this?" I asked Blood.

He looked at it, sniffed it.

"Must be an identity card of some kind. Maybe it's what she used to get out of the downunder."

That made my mind up.

I jammed it in a pocket and started out. Toward the access dropshaft.

"Where the hell are you going?" Blood yelled after me. "Come on back, you'll get killed out there!

"I'm hungry, dammit!

"Albert, you sonofabitch! Come back here!"

I kept right on walking. I was gonna find that bitch and brain her. Even if I had to go downunder to find her.

It took me an hour to walk to the access dropshaft leading down to Topeka. I thought I saw Blood following, but hanging back a ways. I didn't give a damn. I was mad.

Then, there it was. A tall, straight, featureless pillar of shining black metal. It was maybe twenty feet in diameter, perfectly flat on top, disappearing straight into the ground. It was a cap, that was all. I walked straight up to it, and fished around in the pocket for that metal card. Then something was tugging at my right pants leg.

"Listen, you moron, you can't go down there!"

I kicked him off, but he came right back.

"Listen to me!"

I turned around and stared at him.

Blood sat down; the powder puffed up around him. "Albert . . ."

40

"My name is Vic, you little egg-sucker."

"Okay, okay, no fooling around. Vic." His tone softened. "Vic. Come on, man." He was trying to get through to me. I was really boiling, but he was trying to make sense. I shrugged, and crouched down beside him.

"Listen, man," Blood said, "this chick has bent you way out of shape. You *know* you can't go down there. It's all square and settled and they know everyone; they hate solos. Enough roverpaks have raided downunders and raped their broads, and stolen their food, they'll have defenses set up. They'll *kill* you, man!"

"What the hell do you care? You're always saying you'd be better off without me." He sagged at that.

"Vic, we've been together almost three years. Good and bad. But this can be the worst. I'm scared, man. Scared you won't come back. And I'm hungry, and I'll have to find some dude who'll take me on . . . and you know most solos are in paks now, I'll be low mutt. I'm not that young any more. And I'm hurt."

I could dig it. He was talking sense. But all I could think of was how that bitch, that Quilla June, had rapped me. And then there were images of her soft tits, and the way she made little sounds when I was in her, and I shook my head, and knew I had to go get even.

"I got to do it, Blood. I got to."

He breathed deep, and sagged a little more. He knew it was useless. "You don't even see what she's done to you, Vic."

I got up. "I'll try to get back quick. Will you wait . . . ?"

He was silent a long while, and I waited. Finally, he said, "For a while. Maybe I'll be here, maybe not."

I understood. I turned around and started walking around the pillar of black metal. Finally, I found a slot in the pillar, and slipped the metal card into it. There was a soft humming sound, then a section of the pillar dilated. I hadn't even seen the lines of the sections. A circle opened and I took a step through. I turned and there was Blood, watching me. We looked at each other, all the while that pillar was humming.

"So long, Vic."

"Take care of yourself, Blood."

"Hurry back."

41

"Do my best."

"Yeah. Right."

Then I turned around and stepped inside. The access portal irised closed behind me.

VII

I should have known. I should have suspected. Sure, every once in a while a chick came up to see what it was like on the surface, what had happened to the cities; sure, it happened. Why I'd believed her when she'd told me, cuddled up beside me in that steaming boiler, that she'd wanted to see what it was like when a girl did it with a man, that all the flicks she'd seen in Topeka were sweet and solid and dull, and the girls in her school'd talked about beaver flicks, and one of them had a little eight-page comic book and she'd read it with wide eyes . . . sure, I'd believed her. It was logical. I should have suspected something when she left that metal i.d. plate behind. It was too easy. Blood'd tried to tell me. Dumb? Yeah!

The second that access iris swirled closed behind me, the humming got louder, and some cool light grew in the walls. Wall. It was a circular compartment with only two sides to the wall: *in*side and *out*side. The wall pulsed up light and the humming got louder, and then the floor I was standing on dilated just the way the outside port had done. But I was standing there, like a mouse in a cartoon, and as long as I didn't look down I was cool, I wouldn't fall.

Then I started settling. Dropped through the floor, the iris closed overhead, I was dropping down the tube, picking up speed but not too much, just dropping steadily. Now I knew what a dropshaft was.

Down and down I went and every once in a while I'd see something like 10 LEV or ANTIPOLL 55 or BREEDERCON or PUMP SE 6 on the wall, and faintly I could make out the sectioning of an iris . . . but I never stopped dropping.

Finally, I dropped all the way to the bottom and there was TOPEKA CITY LIMITS POP. 22,860 on the wall, and I settled down without any strain, bending a little from the knees to cushion the impact, but even that wasn't much.

I used the metal plate again, and the iris—a much bigger one this time—swirled open, and I got my first look at a downunder.

It stretched away in front of me, twenty miles to the dim shining horizon of tin can metal where the wall behind me curved and curved and curved till it made one smooth, encircling circuit and came back around around around to where I stood, staring at it. I was down at the bottom of a big metal tube that stretched up to a ceiling an eighth of a mile overhead, twenty miles across. And in the bottom of that tin can, someone had built a town that looked for all the world like a photo out of one of the water-logged books in the library on the surface. I'd seen a town like this in the books. Just like this. Neat little houses, and curvy little streets, and trimmed lawns, and a business section and everything else that a Topeka would have.

Except a sun, except birds, except clouds, except rain, except snow, except cold, except wind, except ants, except dirt, except mountains, except oceans, except big fields of grain, except stars, except the moon, except forests, except animals running wild, except . . .

Except freedom.

They were canned down here, like dead fish. Canned.

I felt my throat tighten up. I wanted to get out. Out! I started to tremble, my hands were cold and there was sweat on my forehead. This had been insane, coming down here. I had to get out. *Out!*

I turned around, to get back in the dropshaft, and then it grabbed me.

That bitch Quilla June! I shoulda suspected!

The thing was low, and green, and boxlike, and had cables with mittens on the ends instead of arms, and it rolled on tracks, and it grabbed me.

It hoisted me up on its square flat top, holding me with them mittens on the cables, and I couldn't move, except to try kicking at the big glass eye in the front, but it didn't do any good. It didn't bust. The thing was only about four feet high, and my sneakers almost reached the ground, but not quite, and it started moving off into Topeka, hauling me along with it.

People were all over the place. Sitting in rockers on their front porches, raking their lawns, hanging around

43

the gas station, sticking pennies in gumball machines, painting a white stripe down the middle of the road, selling newspapers on a corner, listening to an oompah band on a shell in a park, playing hopscotch and pussy-in-the-corner, polishing a fire engine, sitting on benches reading, washing windows, pruning bushes, tipping hats to ladies, collecting milk bottles in wire carrying racks, grooming horses, throwing a stick for a dog to retrieve, diving into a communal swimming pool, chalking vegetable prices on a slate outside a grocery, walking hand-in-hand with a girl, all of them watching me go past on that metal motherfucker.

I could hear Blood speaking, saying just what he'd said before I'd entered the dropshaft: *It's all square and settled and they know everyone; they hate solos. Enough rover-paks have raided downunders and raped their broads, and stolen their food, they'll have defenses set up. They'll kill you, man!*

Thanks, mutt.

Goodbye.

VIII

The green box tracked through the business section and turned in at a shopfront with the words BETTER BUSINESS BUREAU on the window. It rolled right inside the open door, and there were half a dozen men and old men and very old men in there, waiting for me. Also a couple of women. The green box stopped.

One of them came over and took the metal plate out of my hand. He looked at it, then turned around and gave it to the oldest of the old men, a withered cat wearing baggy pants and a green eyeshade and garters that held up the sleeves of his striped shirt. "Quilla June, Lew," the guy said to the old man. Lew took the metal plate and put it in the top left drawer of a rolltop desk. "Better take his guns, Aaron," the old coot said. And the guy who'd taken the plate cleaned me.

"Let him loose, Aaron," Lew said.

Aaron stepped around the back of the green box and something clicked, and the cable-mittens sucked back inside the box, and I got down off the thing. My arms were numb where the box had held me. I rubbed one, then the other, and I glared at them.

"Now, boy . . ." Lew started.

"Suck wind, asshole!"

The women blanched. The men tightened their faces.

"I told you it wouldn't work," another of the old men said to Lew.

"Bad business, this," said one of the younger ones.

Lew leaned forward in his straight-back chair and pointed a crumbled finger at me. "Boy, you better be nice."

"I hope all your fuckin' children are hare-lipped!"

"This is no good, Lew!" another man said.

"Guttersnipe," a woman with a beak snapped.

Lew stared at me. His mouth was a nasty little black line. I knew the sonofabitch didn't have a tooth in his crummy head that wasn't rotten and smelly. He stared at me with vicious little eyes, God he was ugly, like a bird ready to pick meat off my bones. He was getting set to say something I wouldn't like. "Aaron, maybe you'd better put the sentry back on him." Aaron moved to the green box.

"Okay, hold it," I said, holding up my hand.

Aaron stopped, looked at Lew, who nodded. Then Lew leaned forward again, and aimed that bird-claw at me. "You ready to behave yourself, son?"

"Yeah, I guess."

"You'd better be dang sure."

"Okay. I'm *dang* sure. Also *fuckin'* sure!"

"And you'll watch your mouth."

I didn't reply. Old coot.

"You're a bit of an experiment for us, boy. We tried to get one of you down here other ways. Sent up some good folks to capture one of you little scuts, but they never came back. Figgered it was best to lure you down to us."

I sneered. That Quilla June. I'd take care of her!

One of the women, a little younger than Bird-Beak, came forward and looked into my face. "Lew, you'll never get this one to kow-tow. He's a filthy little killer. Look at those eyes."

"How'd you like the barrel of a rifle jammed up your ass, bitch?" She jumped back. Lew was angry again.

45

"Sorry," I said, "I don't like bein' called names. *Macho,* y'know?"

He settled back and snapped at the woman. "Mez, leave him alone. I'm tryin' to talk a bit of sense here. You're only making it worse."

Mez went back and sat with the others. Some Better Business Bureau these creeps were!

"As I was saying, boy: you're an experiment for us. We've been down here in Topeka close to twenty years. It's nice down here. Quiet, orderly, nice people who respect each other, no crime, respect for the elders, and just all around a good place to live. We're growin' and we're prosperin'."

I waited.

"But, well, we find now that some of our folks can't have no more babies, and the women that do, they have mostly girls. We need some men. Certain special kind of men."

I started laughing. This was too good to be true. They wanted me for stud service. I couldn't stop laughing.

"Crude!" one of the women said, scowling.

"This's awkward enough for us, boy, don't make it no harder." Lew was embarrassed.

Here I'd spent most of Blood's and my time aboveground hunting up tail, and down here they wanted me to service the local ladyfolk. I sat down on the floor and laughed till tears ran down my cheeks.

Finally, I got up and said, "Sure. Okay. But if I do, there's a couple of things I want."

Lew looked at me close.

"The first thing I want is that Quilla June. I'm gonna fuck her blind, and then I'm gonna bang her on the head the way she did me!"

They huddled for a while, then came out and Lew said, "We can't tolerate any violence down here, but I s'pose Quilla June's as good a place to start as any. She's capable, isn't she, Ira?"

A skinny, yellow-skinned man nodded. He didn't look happy about it. Quilla June's old man, I bet.

"Well, let's get started," I said. "Line 'em up," I started to unzip my jeans.

The women screamed, the men grabbed me, and they hustled me off to a boarding house where they gave me a room, and they said I should get to know Topeka a little bit before I went to work, because it was, uh, er, well, awkward, and they had to get the folks in town to accept what was going to have to be done . . . on the assumption, I suppose, that if I worked out okay, they'd import a few more young bulls from aboveground, and turn us loose.

So I spent some time in Topeka, getting to know the folks, seeing what they did, how they lived. It was nice, real nice. They rocked in rockers on the front porches, they raked their lawns, they hung around the gas station, they stuck pennies in gumball machines, they painted white stripes down the middle of the road, they sold newspapers on the corners, they listened to oompah bands on a shell in the park, they played hopscotch and pussy-in-the-corner, they polished fire engines, they sat on benches reading, they washed windows and pruned bushes, they tipped their hats to ladies, they collected milk bottles in wire carrying racks, they groomed horses and threw sticks for their dogs to retrieve, they dove into the communal swimming pool, they chalked vegetable prices on a slate outside the grocery, they walked hand-in-hand with some of the ugliest chicks I've ever seen, and they bored the ass off me.

Inside a week I was ready to scream.

I could feel that tin can closing in on me.

I could feel the weight of the earth over me.

They ate artificial shit: artificial peas and fake meat and make-believe chicken and ersatz corn and bogus bread and it all tasted like chalk and dust to me.

Polite? Christ, you could puke from the lying, hypocritical crap they called civility. Hello Mr. This and Mrs. That. And how are you? And how is little Janie? And how is business? And are you going to the sodality meeting Thursday? And I started gibbering in my room at the boarding house.

The clean, sweet, neat, lovely way they lived was enough to kill a guy. No wonder the men couldn't get it up and make babies that had balls instead of slots.

The first few days, everyone watched me like I was about to explode and cover their nice whitewashed fences with shit. But after a while, they got used to seeing me. Lew took me over to the mercantile, and got me fitted out with a pair of bib overalls and a shirt that any solo could've spotted a mile away. That Mez, that dippy bitch who'd called me a killer, she started hanging around, finally said she wanted to cut my hair, make me look civilized. But I was hip to where she was at. Wasn't a bit of the mother in her.

"What's'a'matter, cunt," I pinned her. "Your old man isn't taking care of you?"

She tried to stick her fist in her mouth, and I laughed like a loon. "Go cut off his balls, baby. My hair stays the way it is." She cut and run. Went like she had a diesel tail-pipe.

It went on like that for a while. Me just walking around, them coming and feeding me, keeping all their young meat out of my way till they got the town stacked-away for what was coming with me.

Jugged like that, my mind wasn't right for a while. I got all claustrophobed, clutched, went and sat under the porch in the dark, at the rooming house. Then that passed, and I got piss-mean, snapped at them, then surly, then quiet, then just mud dull. Quiet.

Finally, I started getting hip to the possibilities of getting out of there. It began with me remembering the poodle I'd fed Blood one time. It had to of come from a downunder. And it couldn't of got up through the drop-shaft. So that meant there were other ways out.

They gave me pretty much the run of the town, as long as I kept my manners around me and didn't try anything sudden. That green sentry box was always somewhere nearby.

So I found the way out. Nothing so spectacular; it just had to be there, and I found it.

Then I found out where they kept my weapons, and I was ready. Almost.

IX

It was a week to the day when Aaron and Lew and Ira came to get me. I was pretty goofy by that time. I was sitting out on the back porch of the boarding house, smoking a corncob pipe with my shirt off, catching some sun. Except there wasn't no sun. Goofy.

They came around the house. "Morning, Vic," Lew

greeted me. He was hobbling along with a cane, the old fart. Aaron gave me a big smile. The kind you'd give a big black bull about to stuff his meat into a good breed cow. Ira had a look that you could chip off and use in your furnace.

"Well, howdy, Lew. Mornin' Aaron, Ira."

Lew seemed right pleased by that.

Oh, you lousy bastards, just you wait!

"You bout ready to go meet your first lady?"

"Ready as I'll ever be, Lew," I said, and got up.

"Cool smoke, isn't it?" Aaron said.

I took the corncob out of my mouth. "Pure dee-light," I smiled. I hadn't even lit the fucking thing.

They walked me over to Marigold Street and as we came up on a little house with yellow shutters and a white picket fence, Lew said, "This's Ira's house. Quilla June is his daughter."

"Well, land sakes," I said, wide-eyed.

Ira's lean jaw muscles jumped.

We went inside.

Quilla June was sitting on the settee with her mother, an older version of her, pulled thin as a withered muscle. "Miz Holmes," I said, and made a little curtsey. She smiled. Strained, but smiled.

Quilla June sat with her feet right together, and her hands folded in her lap. There was a ribbon in her hair. It was blue.

Matched her eyes.

Something went thump in my gut.

"Quilla June," I said.

She looked up. "Mornin', Vic."

Then everyone sort of stood around looking awkward, and finally Ira began yapping and yipping about get in the bedroom and get this unnatural filth over with so they could go to Church and pray the Good Lord wouldn't Strike All Of Them Dead with a bolt of lightning in the ass, or some crap like that.

So I put out my hand, and Quilla June reached for it without looking up, and we went in the back, into a small bedroom, and she stood there with her head down.

"You didn't tell 'em, did you?" I asked.

She shook her head.

And suddenly, I didn't want to kill her at all. I wanted

49

to hold her. Very tight. So I did. And she was crying into my chest, and making little fists and beating on my back, and then she was looking up at me and running her words all together: "Oh, Vic, I'm sorry, so sorry, I didn't mean to, I had to, I was sent out to, I was so scared, and I love you and now they've got you down here, and it isn't dirty, is it, it isn't the way my Poppa says it is, is it?"

I held her and kissed her and told her it was okay, and then I asked her if she wanted to come away with me, and she said yes yes yes she really did. So I told her I might have to hurt her Poppa to get away, and she got a look in her eyes that I knew real well.

For all her propriety, Quilla June Holmes didn't much like her prayer-shouting Poppa.

I asked her if she had anything heavy, like a candlestick or a club, and she said no. So I went rummaging around in that back bedroom, and found a pair of her Poppa's socks, in a bureau drawer. I pulled the big brass balls off the headboard of the bed, and dropped them into the sock. I hefted it. Oh. Yeah.

She stared at me with big eyes. "What're you going to do?"

"You want to get out of here?"

She nodded.

"Then just stand back behind the door. No, wait a minute, I got a better idea. Get on the bed."

She laid down on the bed. "Okay," I said, "now pull up your skirt, pull off your pants, and spread out." She gave me a look of pure horror. "Do it," I said. "If you want out."

So she did it, and I rearranged her so her knees were bent and her legs open at the thighs, and I stood to one side of the door, and whispered to her, "Call your Poppa. Just him."

She hesitated a long moment, then she called out, in a voice she didn't have to fake, "Poppa! Poppa! Poppa, come here please!" Then she clamped her eyes shut tight.

Ira Holmes came through the door, took one look at his secret desire, his mouth dropped open, I kicked the door closed behind him and walloped him as hard as I could. He squished a little, and spattered the bedspread, and went very down.

She opened her eyes when she heard the thunk! and
50

when the stuff splattered her legs she leaned over and puked on the floor. I knew she wouldn't be much good to me in getting Aaron into the room, so I opened the door, stuck my head around, looked worried, and said, "Aaron, would you come here a minute, please?" He looked at Lew, who was rapping with Mrs. Holmes about what was going on in the back bedroom, and when Lew nodded him on, he came into the room. He took a look at Quilla June's naked bush, at the blood on the wall and bedspread, at Ira on the floor, and opened his mouth to yell, just as I whacked him. It took two more to get him down, and then I had to kick him in the chest to put him away. Quilla June was still puking.

I grabbed her by the arm and swung her up off the bed. At least she was being quiet about it, but man did she stink.

"Come on!"

She tried to pull back, but I held on, and opened the bedroom door. As I pulled her out, Lew stood up, leaning on his cane. I kicked the cane out from under the old fart and down he went in a heap. Mrs. Holmes was staring at us, wondering where her old man was: "He's back in there," I said, heading for the front door. "The Good Lord got him in the head."

Then we were out in the street, Quilla June stinking along behind me, dry-heaving and bawling and probably wondering what had happened to her underpants.

They kept my weapons in a locked case at the Better Business Bureau, and we detoured around by my boarding house where I pulled the crowbar I'd swiped from the gas station out from under the back porch. Then we cut across behind the Grange and into the business section, and straight into the BBB. There was a clerk who tried to stop me, and I split his gourd with the crowbar. Then I pried the latch off the cabinet in Lew's office, and got the .30-06 and my .45 and all the ammo, and my spike, and my knife, and my kit, and loaded up. By that time Quilla June was able to make some sense.

"Where we gonna go, where we gonna go, oh Poppa Poppa Poppa . . . !"

"Hey, listen, Quilla June, Poppa me no Poppas. You said you wanted to be with me . . . well, I'm goin! *up,* baby, and if you wanna go with me, you better stick close."

She was too scared to object.

I stepped out the front of the shopfront, and there was that green box sentry, coming on like a whippet. It had its cables out, and the mittens were gone. It had hooks.

I dropped to one knee, wrapped the sling of the .30-06 around my forearm, sighted clean, and fired dead at the big eye in the front. One shot, spang!

Hit that eye, the thing exploded in a shower of sparks, and the green box swerved and went through the front window of The Mill End Shoppe, screeching and crying and showering the place with flames and sparks. Nice.

I turned around to grab Quilla June, but she was gone. I looked off down the street, and here came all the vigilantes, Lew hobbling along with his cane like some kind of weird grasshopper.

And right then the shots started. Big, booming sounds. The .45 I'd given Quilla June. I looked up, and on the porch around the second floor, there she was, the automatic down on the railing like a pro, sighting into that mob and snapping off shots like maybe Wild Bill Elliott in a 40's Republic flick.

But dumb! Mother, dumb! Wasting time on that, when we had to get away.

I found the outside staircase going up there, and took it three steps at a time. She was smiling and laughing, and every time she'd pick one of those boobs out of the pack her little tongue-tip would peek out of the corner of her mouth, and her eyes would get all slick and wet and wham! down the boob would go.

She was really into it.

Just as I reached her, she sighted down on her scrawny mother. I slammed the back of her head and she missed the shot, and the old lady did a little dance-step and kept coming. Quilla June whipped her head around at me, and there was kill in her eyes. "You made me miss." The voice gave me a chill.

I took the .45 away from her. Dumb. Wasting ammunition like that.

Dragging her behind me, I circled the building, found a shed out back, dropped down onto it and had her follow. She was scared at first, but I said, "Chick can shoot her old lady as easy as you do shouldn't be worried about a drop this small." She got out on the edge, other side of the railing and held on. "Don't worry," I said, "you won't wet your pants. You haven't got any."

She laughed, like a bird, and dropped. I caught her, we slid down the shed door, and took a second to see if that mob was hard on us. Nowhere in sight.

I grabbed Quilla June by the arm and started off toward the south end of Topeka. It was the closest exit I'd found in my wandering, and we made it in about fifteen minutes, panting and weak as kittens.

And there it was.

A big air-intake duct.

I pried off the clamps with the crowbar, and we climbed up inside. There were ladders going up. There had to be. It figured. Repairs. Keep it clean. Had to be. We started climbing.

It took a long, long time.

Quilla June kept asking me, from down behind me, whenever she got too tired to climb, "Vic, do you love me?" I kept saying yes. Not only because I meant it. It helped her keep climbing.

X

We came up a mile from the access dropshaft. I shot off the filter covers and the hatch bolts, and we climbed out. They should have known better down there. You don't fuck around with Jimmy Cagney.

They never had a chance.

Quilla June was exhausted. I didn't blame her. But I didn't want to spend the night out in the open; there were things out there I didn't like to think about meeting even in daylight. It was getting on toward dusk.

We walked toward the access dropshaft.

Blood was waiting.

He looked weak. But he'd waited.

I stooped down and lifted his head. He opened his eyes, and very softly he said, "Hey."

I smiled at him. Jesus, it was good to see him. "We made it back, man."

He tried to get up, but he couldn't. The wounds on him were in ugly shape. "Have you eaten?" I asked.

"No. Grabbed a lizard yesterday . . . or maybe it was day before. I'm hungry, Vic."

Quilla June came up then, and Blood saw her. He closed his eyes. "We'd better hurry, Vic," she said. "Please. They might come up from the dropshaft."

I tried to lift Blood. He was dead weight. "Listen, Blood, I'll leg it into the city and get some food. I'll come back quick. You just wait here."

"Don't go in there, Vic," he said. "I did a recon the day after you went down. They found out we weren't fried in that gym. I don't know how. Maybe mutts smelled our track. I've been keeping watch, and they haven't tried to come out after us. I don't blame them. You don't know what it's like out here at night, man . . . you don't know . . ."

He shivered.

"Take it easy, Blood."

"But they've got us marked lousy in the city, Vic. We can't go back there. We'll have to make it someplace else."

That put it on a different stick. We couldn't go back, and with Blood in that condition we couldn't go forward. And I knew, good as I was solo, I couldn't make it without him. And there wasn't anything out here to eat. He had to have food, at once, and some medical care. I had to do something. Something good, something fast.

"Vic," Quilla June's voice was high and whining, "come *on!* He'll be all right. We have to hurry."

I looked up at her. The sun was going down. Blood trembled in my arms.

She got a pouty look on her face. "If you love me, you'll come *on!*"

I couldn't make it alone out there without him. I knew it. If I loved her. She asked me, in the boiler, do you know what love is?

It was a small fire, not nearly big enough for any roverpak to spot from the outskirts of the city. No smoke. And after Blood had eaten his fill, I carried him to the airduct a mile away, and we spent the night inside, on a little ledge. I held him all night. He slept good. In the morning, I fixed him up pretty good. He'd make it; he was strong.

54

He ate again. There was plenty left from the night before. I didn't eat. I wasn't hungry.

We started off across the blast wasteland that morning. We'd find another city, and make it.

We had to move slow, because Blood was still limping. It took a long time before I stopped hearing her calling in my head. Asking me, asking me: *do you know what love is?*

Sure I know.

A boy loves his dog.

*This story appeared so late in 1969 that it only just qualified
as a candidate, but placed second in its category all the same.
It is easy to see why. It is "hard" science fiction; it is elegantly
written; and it makes, God bless it, a serious philosophical
point which could have been made in no other way. It
appeared in* Playboy, *by the way, with the authoress' first
name truncated to an initial.*

NINE LIVES

Ursula K. Le Guin

She was alive inside but dead outside, her face a black
and dun net of wrinkles, tumors, cracks. She was bald
and blind. The tremors that crossed Libra's face were
mere quiverings of corruption: underneath, in the black
corridors, the halls beneath the skin, there were crepita-
tions in darkness, ferments, chemical nightmares that went
on for centuries. "Oh the damned flatulent planet," Pugh
murmured as the dome shook and a boil burst a kilometer
to the southwest, spraying silver pus across the sunset.
The sun had been setting for the last two days. "I'll be
glad to see a human face."

"Thanks," said Martin.

"Yours is human to be sure," said Pugh, "but I've seen
it so long I can't see it."

Radvid signals cluttered the communicator which Martin was operating, faded, returned as face and voice. The
face filled the screen, the nose of an Assyrian king, the eyes
of a samurai, skin bronze, eyes the color of iron: young,
magnificent. "Is that what human beings look like?" said
Pugh with awe. "I'd forgotten."

56

"Shut up, Owen, we're on."

"Libra Exploratory Mission Base, come in please, this is *Passerine* launch."

"Libra here. Beam fixed. Come on down, launch."

"Expulsion in seven E-seconds. Hold on." The screen blanked and sparkled.

"Do they all look like that? Martin, you and I are uglier men than I thought."

"Shut up, Owen. . . ."

For twenty-two minutes Martin followed the landing-craft down by signal and then through the cleared dome they saw it, small star in the blood-colored east, sinking. It came down neat and quiet, Libra's thin atmosphere carrying little sound. Pugh and Martin closed the head-pieces of their imsuits, zipped out of the dome airlocks, and ran with soaring strides, Nijinsky and Nureyev, to-ward the boat. Three equipment modules came floating down at four-minute intervals from each other and hun-dred-meter intervals east of the boat. "Come on out," Martin said on his suit radio, "we're waiting at the door."

"Come on in, the methane's fine," said Pugh.

The hatch opened. The young man they had seen on the screen came out with one athletic twist and leaped down onto the shaky dust and clinkers of Libra. Martin shook his hand, but Pugh was staring at the hatch, from which another young man emerged with the same neat twist and jump, followed by a young woman who emerged with the same neat twist, ornamented by a wriggle, and the jump. They were all tall, with bronze skin, black hair, high-bridged nose, epicanthic fold, the same face. They all had the same face. The fourth was emerging from the hatch with a neat twist and jump. "Martin bach," said Pugh, "we've got a clone."

"Right," said one of them, "we're a tenclone. John Chow's the name. You're Lieutenant Martin?"

"I'm Owen Pugh."

"Alvare Guillen Martin," said Martin, formal, bowing slightly. Another girl was out, the same beautiful face; Martin stared at her and his eye rolled like a nervous pony's. Evidently he had never given any thought to cloning, and was suffering technological shock. "Steady," Pugh said in the Argentine dialect, "it's only excess twins."

He stood close by Martin's elbow. He was glad himself of the contact.

It is hard to meet a stranger. Even the greatest extrovert meeting even the meekest stranger knows a certain dread, though he may not know he knows it. Will he make a fool of me wreck my image of myself invade me destroy me change me? Will he be different from me? Yes, that he will. There's the terrible thing: the strangeness of the stranger.

After two years on a dead planet, and the last half year isolated as a team of two, oneself and one other, after that it's even harder to meet a stranger, however welcome he may be. You're out of the habit of difference, you've lost the touch; and so the fear revives, the primitive anxiety, the old dread.

The clone, five males and five females, had got done in a couple of minutes what a man might have got done in twenty: greeted Pugh and Martin, had a glance at Libra, unloaded the boat, made ready to go. They went, and the dome filled with them, a hive of golden bees. They hummed and buzzed quietly, filled up all silences, all spaces with a honey-brown swarm of human presence. Martin looked bewilderedly at the long-limbed girls, and they smiled at him, three at once. Their smile was gentler than that of the boys, but no less radiantly self-possessed.

"Self-possessed," Owen Pugh murmured to his friend. "That's it. Think of it, to be oneself ten times over. Nine seconds for every motion, nine ayes on every vote. It would be glorious!" But Martin was asleep. And the John Chows had all gone to sleep at once. The dome was filled with their quiet breathing. They were young, they didn't snore. Martin sighed and snored, his hershey-bar-colored face relaxed in the dim afterglow of Libra's primary, set at last. Pugh had cleared the dome and stars looked in, Sol among them, a great company of lights, a clone of splendors. Pugh slept and dreamed of a one-eyed giant who chased him through the shaking halls of Hell.

From his sleeping-bag Pugh watched the clone's awakening. They all got up within one minute except for one pair, a boy and a girl, who lay snugly tangled and still sleeping in one bag. As Pugh saw this there was a shock like one of Libra's earthquakes inside him, a very deep

58

tremor. He was not aware of this, and in fact thought he was pleased at the sight; there was no other such comfort on this dead hollow world, more power to them, who made love. One of the others stepped on the pair. They woke and the girl sat up flushed and sleepy, with bare golden breasts. One of her sisters murmured something to her; she shot a glance at Pugh and disappeared in the sleeping-bag, followed by a faint giggle, from another direction a fierce stare, from still another direction a voice: "Christ, we're used to having a room to ourselves. Hope you don't mind, Captain Pugh."

"It's a pleasure," Pugh said half-truthfully. He had to stand up then, wearing only the shorts he slept in, and he felt like a plucked rooster, all white scrawn and pimples. He had seldom envied Martin's compact brownness so much. The United Kingdom had come through the Great Famines well, losing less than half its population: a record achieved by rigorous food-control. Blackmarketeers and hoarders had been executed. Crumbs had been shared. Where in richer lands most had died and a few had thriven, in Britain fewer died and none throve. They all got lean. Their sons were lean, their grandsons lean, small, brittle-boned, easily infected. When civilization became a matter of standing in lines, the British had kept queue, and so had replaced the survival of the fittest with the survival of the fair-minded. Owen Pugh was a scrawny little man. All the same, he was there.

At the moment he wished he wasn't.

At breakfast a John said, "Now if you'll brief us, Captain Pugh—"

"Owen, then."

"Owen, we can work out our schedule. Anything new on the mine since your last report to your Mission? We saw your reports when *Passerine* was orbiting Planet V, where they are now."

Martin did not answer, though the mine was his discovery and project, and Pugh had to do his best. It was hard to talk to them. The same faces, each with the same expression of intelligent interest, all leaned toward him across the table at almost the same angle. They all nodded together.

Over the Exploitation Corps insignia on their tunics each had a nameband, first name John and last name

Chow of course, but the middle names different. The men were Aleph, Kaph, Yod, Gimel, and Samedh; the women Sadhe, Daleth, Zayin, Beth, and Resh. Pugh tried to use the names but gave it up at once; he could not even tell sometimes which one had spoken, for the voices were all alike.

Martin buttered and chewed his toast, and finally interrupted: "You're a team. Is that it?"

"Right," said two Johns.

"God, what a team! I hadn't seen the point. How much do you each know what the others are thinking?"

"Not at all, properly speaking," replied one of the girls, Zayin. The others watched her with the proprietary, approving look they had. "No ESP, nothing fancy. But we think alike. We have exactly the same equipment. Given the same stimulus, the same problem, we're likely to be coming up with the same reactions and solutions at the same time. Explanations are easy—don't even have to make them, usually. We seldom misunderstand each other. It does facilitate our working as a team."

"Christ yes," said Martin. "Pugh and I have spent seven hours out of ten for six months misunderstanding each other. Like most people. What about emergencies, are you as good at meeting the unexpected problem as a nor . . . an unrelated team?"

"Statistics so far indicate that we are," Zayin answered readily. Clones must be trained, Pugh thought, to meet questions, to reassure and reason. All they said had the slightly bland and stilted quality of answers furnished to the Public. "We can't brainstorm as singletons can, we as a team don't profit from the interplay of varied minds; but we have a compensatory advantage. Clones are drawn from the best human material, individuals of IIQ 99th percentile, Genetic Constitution alpha double A, and so on. We have more to draw on than most individuals do."

"And it's multiplied by a factor of ten. Who is—who was John Chow?"

"A genius surely," Pugh said politely. His interest in cloning was not so new and avid as Martin's.

"Leonardo Complex type," said Yod. "Biomath, also a cellist, and an undersea hunter, and interested in structural engineering problems, and so on. Died before he'd worked out his major theories."

60

"Then you each represent a different facet of his mind, his talents?"

"No," said Zayin, shaking her head in time with several others. "We share the basic equipment and tendencies, of course, but we're all engineers in Planetary Exploitation. A later clone can be trained to develop other aspects of the basic equipment. It's all training; the genetic substance is identical. We *are* John Chow. But we were differently trained."

Martin looked shell-shocked. "How old are you?"

"Twenty-three."

"You say he died young— Had they taken germ cells from him beforehand or something?"

Gimel took over: "He died at twenty-four in an aircar crash. They couldn't save the brain, so they took some intestinal cells and cultured them for cloning. Reproductive cells aren't used for cloning since they have only half the chromosomes. Intestinal cells happen to be easy to despecialize and reprogram for total growth."

"All chips off the old block," Martin said valiantly. "But how can . . . some of you be women . . . ?"

Beth took over: "It's easy to program half the clonal mass back to the female. Just delete the male gene from half the cells and they revert to the basic, that is, the female. It's trickier to go the other way, have to hook in artificial Y chromosomes. So they mostly clone from males, since clones function best bisexually."

Gimel again: "They've worked these matters of technique and function out carefully. The taxpayer wants the best for his money, and of course clones are expensive. With the cell-manipulations, and the incubation in Ngama Placentae, and the maintenance and training of the foster-parent groups, we end up costing about three million apiece."

"For your next generation," Martin said, still struggling, "I suppose you . . . you breed?"

"We females are sterile," said Beth with perfect equanimity; "you remember that the Y chromosome was deleted from our original cell. The males can interbreed with approved singletons, if they want to. But to get John Chow again as often as they want, they just reclone a cell from this clone."

Martin gave up the struggle. He nodded and chewed

61

cold toast. "Well," said one of the Johns, and all changed mood, like a flock of starlings that change course in one wingflick, following a leader so fast that no eye can see which leads. They were ready to go. "How about a look at the mine? Then we'll unload the equipment. Some nice new models in the roboats; you'll want to see them. Right?" Had Pugh or Martin not agreed they might have found it hard to say so. The Johns were polite but unanimous; their decisions carried. Pugh, Commander of Libra Base 2, felt a qualm. Could he boss around this superman-woman-entity-of-ten? and a genius at that? He stuck close to Martin as they suited for outside. Neither said anything.

Four apiece in the three large jetsleds, they slipped off north from the dome, over Libra's dun rugose skin, in starlight.

"Desolate," one said.

It was a boy and girl with Pugh and Martin. Pugh wondered if these were the two that had shared a sleeping-bag last night. No doubt they wouldn't mind if he asked them. Sex must be as handy as breathing, to them. Did you two breathe last night?

"Yes," he said, "it is desolate."

"This is our first time Off, except training on Luna." The girl's voice was definitely a bit higher and softer.

"How did you take the big hop?"

"They doped us. I wanted to experience it." That was the boy; he sounded wistful. They seemed to have more personality, only two at a time. Did repetition of the individual negate individuality?

"Don't worry," said Martin, steering the sled, "you can't experience no-time because it isn't there."

"I'd just like to once," one of them said. "So we'd know."

The Mountains of Merioneth showed leprotic in starlight to the east, a plume of freezing gas trailed silvery from a vent-hole to the west, and the sled tilted groundward. The twins braced for the stop at one moment, each with a slight protective gesture to the other. Your skin is my skin, Pugh thought, but literally, no metaphor. What would it be like, then, to have someone as close to you as that? Always to be answered when you spoke, never to be in pain alone. Love your neighbor as you love yourself . . . That hard old problem was solved. The neighbor was the self: the love was perfect.

And here was Hellmouth, the mine.

Pugh was the Exploratory Mission's ET geologist, and Martin his technician and cartographer; but when in the course of a local survey Martin had discovered the U-mine, Pugh had given him full credit, as well as the onus of prospecting the lode and planning the Exploitation team's job. These kids had been sent out from Earth years before Martin's reports got there, and had not known what their job would be until they got here. The Exploitation Corps simply sent out teams regularly and blindly as a dandelion sends out its seeds, knowing there would be a job for them on Libra or the next planet out or one they hadn't even heard about yet. The Government wanted uranium too urgently to wait while reports drifted home across the light-years. The stuff was like gold, old-fashioned but essential, worth mining extraterrestrially and shipping interstellar. Worth its weight in people, Pugh thought sourly, watching the tall young men and women go one by one, glimmering in starlight, into the black hole Martin had named Hellmouth.

As they went in their homeostatic forehead-lamps brightened. Twelve nodding gleams ran along the moist, wrinkled walls. Pugh heard Martin's radiation counter peeping twenty to the dozen up ahead. "Here's the drop-off," said Martin's voice in the suit intercom, drowning out the peeping and the dead silence that was around them. "We're in a side-fissure; this is the main vertical vent in front of us." The black void gaped, its far side not visible in the headlamp beams. "Last vulcanism seems to have been a couple of thousand years ago. Nearest fault is twenty-eight kilos east, in the Trench. This region seems to be as safe seismically as anything in the area. The big basalt-flow overhead stabilizes all these substructures, so long as it remains stable itself. Your central lode is thirty-six meters down and runs in a series of five bubble-caverns northeast. It is a lode, a pipe of very high-grade ore. You saw the percentage figures, right? Extraction's going to be no problem. All you've got to do is get the bubbles topside."

"Take off the lid and let 'em float up." A chuckle. Voices began to talk, but they were all the same voice

63

and the suit radio gave them no location in space. "Open the thing right up. —Safer that way. —But it's a solid basalt roof, how thick, ten meters here? —Three to twenty, the report said. —Blow good ore all over the lot. —Use this access we're in, straighten it a bit and run slider-rails for the robos. —Import burros. —Have we got enough propping material? —What's your estimate of total payload mass, Martin?"

"Say over five million kilos and under eight."

"Transport will be here in ten E-months. —It'll have to go pure. —No, they'll have the mass problem in NAFAL shipping licked by now; remember it's been sixteen years since we left Earth last Tuesday. —Right, they'll send the whole lot back and purify it in Earth orbit. —Shall we go down, Martin?"

"Go on. I've been down."

The first one—Aleph? (Heb., the ox, the leader)— swung onto the ladder and down; the rest followed. Pugh and Martin stood at the chasm's edge. Pugh set his intercom to exchange only with Martin's suit, and noticed Martin doing the same. It was a bit wearing, this listening to one person think aloud in ten voices, or was it one voice speaking the thoughts of ten minds?

"A great gut," Pugh said, looking down into the black pit, its veined and warted walls catching stray gleams of headlamps far below. "A cow's bowel. A bloody great constipated intestine."

Martin's counter peeped like a lost chicken. They stood inside the epileptic planet, breathing oxygen from tanks, wearing suits impermeable to corrosives and harmful radiations, resistant to a two-hundred-degree range of temperatures, tear-proof, and as shock-resistant as possible given the soft vulnerable stuff inside.

"Next hop," Martin said, "I'd like to find a planet that has nothing whatever to exploit."

"You found this."

"Keep me home next time."

Pugh was pleased. He had hoped Martin would want to go on working with him, but neither of them was used to talking much about their feelings, and he had hesitated to ask. "I'll try that," he said.

"I hate this place. I like caves, you know. It's why I came in here. Just spelunking. But this one's a bitch.

Mean. You can't ever let down in here. I guess this lot can handle it, though. They know their stuff."

"Wave of the future, whatever," said Pugh.

The wave of the future came swarming up the ladder, swept Martin to the entrance, gabbled at and around him: "Have we got enough material for supports? —If we convert one of the extractor-servos to anneal, yes. —Sufficient if we miniblast? —Kaph can calculate stress."

Pugh had switched his intercom back to receive them; he looked at them, so many thoughts jabbering in an eager mind, and at Martin standing silent among them, and at Hellmouth, and the wrinkled plain. "Settled! How does that strike you as a preliminary schedule, Martin?"

"It's your baby," Martin said.

Within five E-days the Johns had all their material and equipment unloaded and operating, and were starting to open up the mine. They worked with total efficiency. Pugh was fascinated and frightened by their effectiveness, their confidence, their independence. He was no use to them at all. A clone, he thought, might indeed be the first truly stable, self-reliant human being. Once adult it would need nobody's help. It would be sufficient to itself physically, sexually, emotionally, intellectually. Whatever he did, any member of it would always receive the support and approval of his peers, his other selves. Nobody else was needed.

Two of the clone stayed in the dome doing calculations and paperwork, with frequent sled-trips to the mine for measurements and tests. They were the mathematicians of the clone, Zayin and Kaph. That is, as Zayin explained, all ten had had thorough mathematical training from age three to twenty-one, but from twenty-one to twenty-three she and Kaph had gone on with math while the others intensified other specialties, geology, mining engineering, electronic engineering, equipment robotics, applied atomics, and so on. "Kaph and I feel," she said, "that we're the element of the clone closest to what John Chow was in his singleton lifetime. But of course he was principally in biomath, and they didn't take us far in that,"

"They needed us most in this field," Kaph said, with the patriotic priggishness they sometimes evinced.

Pugh and Martin soon could distinguish this pair from

the others, Zayin by gestalt, Kaph only by a discolored left fourth fingernail, got from an ill-aimed hammer at the age of six. No doubt there were many such differences, physical and psychological, among them; nature might be identical, nurture could not be. But the differences were hard to find. And part of the difficulty was that they really never talked to Pugh and Martin. They joked with them, were polite, got along fine. They gave nothing. It was nothing one could complain about; they were very pleasant, they had the standardized American friendliness.

"Do you come from Ireland, Owen?"

"Nobody comes from Ireland, Zayin."

"There are lots of Irish-Americans."

"To be sure, but no more Irish. A couple of thousand in all the island, the last I knew. They didn't go in for birth-control, you know, so the food ran out. By the Third Famine there were no Irish left at all but the priesthood, and they were all celibate, or nearly all."

Zayin and Kaph smiled stiffly. They had no experience of either bigotry or irony. "What are you then, ethnically?" Kaph asked, and Pugh replied, "A Welshman."

"It is Welsh that you and Martin speak together?"

None of your business, Pugh thought, but said, "No, it's his dialect, not mine: Argentinean. A descendant of Spanish."

"You learned it for private communication?"

"Whom had we here to be private from? It's just that sometimes a man likes to speak his native language."

"Ours is English," Kaph said unsympathetically. Why should they have sympathy? That's one of the things you give because you need it back.

"Is Wells quaint?" asked Zayin.

"Wells? Oh, Wales, it's called. Yes. Wales is quaint." Pugh switched on his rock-cutter, which prevented further conversation by a synapse-destroying whine, and while it whined he turned his back and said a profane word in Welsh.

That night he used the Argentine dialect for private communication. "Do they pair off in the same couples or change every night?"

Martin looked surprised. A prudish expression, unsuited to his features, appeared for a moment. It faded. He too was curious. "I think it's random."

66

"Don't whisper, man, it sounds dirty. I think they rotate."

"On a schedule?"

"So nobody gets omitted."

Martin gave a vulgar laugh and smothered it. "What about us? Aren't we omitted?"

"That doesn't occur to them."

"What if I proposition one of the girls?"

"She'd tell the others and they'd decide as a group."

"I am not a bull," Martin said, his dark, heavy face heating up. "I will not be judged—"

"Down, down, *machismo*," said Pugh. "Do you mean to proposition one?"

Martin shrugged, sullen. "Let 'em have their incest."

"Incest is it, or masturbation?"

"I don't care, if they'd do it out of earshot!"

The clone's early attempts at modesty had soon worn off, unmotivated by any deep defensiveness of self or awareness of others. Pugh and Martin were daily deeper swamped under the intimacies of its constant emotional-sexual-mental interchange: swamped yet excluded.

"Two months to go," Martin said one evening.

"To what?" snapped Pugh. He was edgy lately and Martin's sullenness got on his nerves.

"To relief."

In sixty days the full crew of their Exploratory Mission were due back from their survey of the other planets of the system. Pugh was aware of this.

"Crossing off the days on your calendar?" he jeered.

"Pull yourself together, Owen."

"What do you mean?"

"What I say."

They parted in contempt and resentment.

Pugh came in after a day alone on the Pampas, a vast lava-plain the nearest edge of which was two hours south by jet. He was tired, but refreshed by solitude. They were not supposed to take long trips alone, but lately had often done so. Martin stooped under bright lights, drawing one of his elegant, masterly charts: this one was of the whole face of Libra, the cancerous face. The dome was otherwise empty, seeming dim and large as it had before the clone came. "Where's the golden horde?"

67

Martin grunted ignorance, crosshatching. He straightened his back to glance around at the sun, which squatted feebly like a great red toad on the eastern plain, and at the clock, which said 18:45. "Some big quakes today," he said, returning to his map. "Feel them down there? Lot of crates were falling around. Take a look at the seismo."

The needle jigged and wavered on the roll. It never stopped dancing here. The roll had recorded five quakes of major intensity back in mid-afternoon; twice the needle had hopped off the roll. The attached computer had been activated to emit a slip reading, "Epicenter 61' N by 42'4" E."

"Not in the Trench this time."

"I thought it felt a bit different from usual. Sharper."

"In Base One I used to lie awake all night feeling the ground jump. Queer how you get used to things."

"Go spla if you didn't. What's for dinner?"

"I thought you'd have cooked it."

"Waiting for the clone."

Feeling put upon, Pugh got out a dozen dinnerboxes, stuck two in the Instobake, pulled them out. "All right, here's dinner."

"Been thinking," Martin said, coming to the table. "What if some clone cloned itself? Illegally. Made a thousand duplicates—ten thousand. Whole army. They could make a tidy power-grab, couldn't they?"

"But how many millions did this lot cost to rear? Artificial placentae and all that. It would be hard to keep secret, unless they had a planet to themselves. . . . Back before the Famines, when Earth had national governments, they talked about that; clone your best soldiers, have whole regiments of them. But the food ran out before they could play that game."

They talked amicably, as they used to do.

"Funny," Martin said, chewing. "They left early this morning, didn't they?"

"All but Kaph and Zayin. They thought they'd get the first payload aboveground today. What's up?"

"They weren't back for lunch."

"They won't starve, to be sure."

"They left at seven."

"So they did." Then Pugh saw it. The air-tanks held eight hours' supply.

"Kaph and Zayin carried out spare cans when they left. Or they've got a heap out there."

"They did, but they brought the whole lot in to recharge." Martin stood up, pointing to one of the stacks of stuff that cut the dome into rooms and alleys.

"There's an alarm signal on every imsuit."

"It's not automatic."

Pugh was tired and still hungry. "Sit down and eat, man. That lot can look after themselves."

Martin sat down, but did not eat. "There was a big quake, Owen. The first one. Big enough, it scared me."

After a pause Pugh sighed and said, "All right."

Unenthusiastically, they got out the two-man sled that was always left for them, and headed it north. The long sunrise covered everything in poisonous red jello. The horizontal light and shadow made it hard to see, raised walls of fake iron ahead of them through which they slid, turned the convex plain beyond Hellmouth into a great dimple full of bloody water. Around the tunnel entrance a wilderness of machinery stood, cranes and cables and servos and wheels and diggers and robocarts and sliders and control-huts, all slanting and bulking incoherently in the red light. Martin jumped from the sled, ran into the mine. He came out again, to Pugh. "Oh God, Owen, it's down," he said. Pugh went in and saw, five meters from the entrance, the shiny, moist, black wall that ended the tunnel. Newly exposed to air, it looked organic, like visceral tissue. The tunnel entrance, enlarged by blasting and double-tracked for robocarts, seemed unchanged until he noticed thousands of tiny spiderweb cracks in the walls. The floor was wet with some sluggish fluid.

"They were inside," Martin said.

"They may be still. They surely had extra aircans—"

"Look, Owen, look at the basalt flow, at the roof; don't you see what the quake did, look at it."

The low hump of land that roofed the caves still had the unreal look of an optical illusion. It had reversed itself, sunk down, leaving a vast dimple or pit. When Pugh walked on it he saw that it too was cracked with many tiny fissures. From some a whitish gas was seeping, so that the sunlight on the surface of the gas-pool was shafted as if by the waters of a dim red lake.

"The mine's not on the fault. There's no fault here!"

Pugh came back to him quickly. "No, there's no fault, Martin. Look, they surely weren't all inside together."

Martin followed him and searched among the wrecked machines dully, then actively. He spotted the airsled. It had come down heading south, and stuck at an angle in a pothole of colloidal dust. It had carried two riders. One was half-sunk in the dust, but his suit-meters registered normal functioning; the other hung strapped onto the tilted sled. Her imsuit had burst open on the broken legs, and the body was frozen hard as any rock. That was all they found. As both regulation and custom demanded, they cremated the dead at once with the laser-guns they carried by regulation and had never used before. Pugh, knowing he was going to be sick, wrestled the survivor onto the two-man sled and sent Martin off to the dome with him. Then he vomited, and flushed the waste out of his suit, and finding one four-man sled undamaged followed after Martin, shaking as if the cold of Libra had got through to him.

The survivor was Kaph. He was in deep shock. They found a swelling on the occiput that might mean concussion, but no fracture was visible.

Pugh brought two glasses of food-concentrate and two chasers of aquavit. "Come on," he said. Martin obeyed, drinking off the tonic. They sat down on crates near the cot and sipped the aquavit.

Kaph lay immobile, face like beeswax, hair bright black to the shoulders, lips stiffly parted for faintly gasping breaths.

"It must have been the first shock, the big one," Martin said. "It must have slid the whole structure sideways. Till it fell in on itself. There must be gas layers in the lateral rocks, like those formations in the Thirty-first Quadrant. But there wasn't any sign—" As he spoke the world slid out from under them. Things leaped and clattered, hopped and jigged, shouted Ha! Ha! Ha! "It was like this at fourteen hours," said Reason shakily in Martin's voice, amidst the unfastening and ruin of the world. But Unreason sat up, as the tumult lessened and things ceased dancing, and screamed aloud.

Pugh leaped across his spilled aquavit and held Kaph down. The muscular body flailed him off. Martin pinned the shoulders down. Kaph screamed, struggled, choked;

his face blackened. "Oxy," Pugh said, and his hand found the right needle in the medical kit as if by homing instinct; while Martin held the mask he struck the needle home to the vagus nerve, restoring Kaph to life.

"Didn't know you knew that stunt," Martin said, breathing hard.

"The Lazarus Jab; my father was a doctor. It doesn't often work," Pugh said. "I want that drink I spilled. Is the quake over? I can't tell."

"Aftershocks. It's not just you shivering."

"Why did he suffocate?"

"I don't know, Owen. Look in the book."

Kaph was breathing normally and his color was restored, only the lips were still darkened. They poured a new shot of courage and sat down by him again with their medical guide. "Nothing about cyanosis or asphyxiation under 'shock' or 'concussion.' He can't have breathed in anything with his suit on. I don't know. We'd get as much good out of *Mother Mog's Home Herbalist* . . . 'Anal Hemorrhoids,' fy!" Pugh pitched the book to a crate-table. It fell short, because either Pugh or the table was still unsteady.

"Why didn't he signal?"

"Sorry?"

"The eight inside the mine never had time. But he and the girl must have been outside. Maybe she was in the entrance, and got hit by the first slide. He must have been outside, in the control-hut maybe. He ran in, pulled her out, strapped her onto the sled, started for the dome. And all that time never pushed the panic button in his imsuit. Why not?"

"Well, he'd had that whack on his head. I doubt he ever realized the girl was dead. He wasn't in his senses. But if he had been I don't know if he'd have thought to signal us. They looked to one another for help."

Martin's face was like an Indian mask, grooves at the mouth-corners, eyes of dull coal. "That's so. What must he have felt, then, when the quake came and he was outside, alone—"

In answer Kaph screamed.

He came up off the cot in the heaving convulsions of one suffocating, knocked Pugh right down with his flailing arm, staggered into a stack of crates and fell to the

71

floor, lips blue, eyes white. Martin dragged him back onto the cot and gave him a whiff of oxygen, then knelt by Pugh, who was just sitting up, and wiped at his cut cheekbone. "Owen, are you all right, are you going to be all right, Owen?"

"I think I am," Pugh said. "Why are you rubbing that on my face?"

It was a short length of computer-tape, now spotted with Pugh's blood. Martin dropped it. "Thought it was a towel. You clipped your cheek on that box there."

"Is he out of it?"

"Seems to be."

They stared down at Kaph lying stiff, his teeth a white line inside dark parted lips.

"Like epilepsy. Brain damage maybe?"

"What about shooting him full of meprobamate?"

Pugh shook his head. "I don't know what's in that shot I already gave him for shock. Don't want to overdose him."

"Maybe he'll sleep it off now."

"I'd like to myself. Between him and the earthquake I can't seem to keep on my feet."

"You got a nasty crack there. Go on, I'll sit up a while."

Pugh cleaned his cut cheek and pulled off his shirt, then paused.

"Is there anything we ought to have done—have tried to do—"

"They're all dead," Martin said heavily, gently.

Pugh lay down on top of his sleeping-bag, and one instant later was wakened by a hideous, sucking, struggling noise. He staggered up, found the needle, tried three times to jab it in correctly and failed, began to massage over Kaph's heart. "Mouth-to-mouth," he said, and Martin obeyed. Presently Kaph drew a harsh breath, his heartbeat steadied, his rigid muscles began to relax.

"How long did I sleep?"

"Half an hour."

They stood up sweating. The ground shuddered, the fabric of the dome sagged and swayed. Libra was dancing her awful polka again, her Totentanz. The sun, though rising, seemed to have grown larger and redder; gas and dust must have been stirred up in the feeble atmosphere.

"What's wrong with him, Owen?"

72

"I think he's dying with them."

"Them— But they're dead, I tell you."

"Nine of them. They're all dead, they were crushed or suffocated. They were all him, he is all of them. They died, and now he's dying their deaths one by one."

"Oh pity of God," said Martin.

The next time was much the same. The fifth time was worse, for Kaph fought and raved, trying to speak but getting no words out, as if his mouth were stopped with rocks or clay. After that the attacks grew weaker, but so did he. The eighth seizure came at about four-thirty; Pugh and Martin worked till five-thirty doing all they could to keep life in the body that slid without protest into death. They kept him, but Martin said, "The next will finish him." And it did; but Pugh breathed his own breath into the inert lungs, until he himself passed out.

He woke. The dome was opaqued and no light on. He listened and heard the breathing of two sleeping men. He slept, and nothing woke him till hunger did.

The sun was well up over the dark plains, and the planet had stopped dancing. Kaph lay asleep. Pugh and Martin drank tea and looked at him with proprietary triumph.

When he woke Martin went to him: "How do you feel, old man?" There was no answer. Pugh took Martin's place and looked into the brown, dull eyes that gazed toward but not into his own. Like Martin he quickly turned away. He heated food-concentrate and brought it to Kaph. "Come on, drink."

He could see the muscles in Kaph's throat tighten. "Let me die," the young man said.

"You're not dying."

Kaph spoke with clarity and precision: "I am nine-tenths dead. There is not enough of me left alive."

That precision convinced Pugh, and he fought the conviction. "No," he said, peremptory. "They are dead. The others. Your brothers and sisters. You're not them, you're alive. You are John Chow. Your life is in your own hands."

The young man lay still, looking into a darkness that was not there.

Martin and Pugh took turns taking the Exploitation hauler and a spare set of robos over to Hellmouth to salvage equipment and protect it from Libra's sinister atmosphere, for the value of the stuff was, literally, astronomical. It was slow work for one man at a time, but they were unwilling to leave Kaph by himself. The one left in the dome did paperwork, while Kaph sat or lay and stared into his darkness, and never spoke. The days went by silent.

The radio spat and spoke: the Mission calling from ship. "We'll be down on Libra in five weeks, Owen. Thirty-four E-days nine hours I make it as of now. How's tricks in the old dome?"

"Not good, chief. The Exploit team were killed, all but one of them, in the mine. Earthquake. Six days ago."

The radio crackled and sang starsong. Sixteen seconds lag each way; the ship was out around Plant III now. "Killed, all but one? You and Martin were unhurt?"

"We're all right, chief."

Thirty-two seconds.

Passerine left an Exploit team out here with us. I may put them on the Hellmouth project then, instead of the Quadrant Seven project. We'll settle that when we come down. In any case you and Martin will be relieved at Dome Two. Hold tight. Anything else?"

"Nothing else."

Thirty-two seconds.

"Right then. So long, Owen."

Kaph had heard all this, and later on Pugh said to him, "The chief may ask you to stay here with the other Exploit team. You know the ropes here." Knowing the exigencies of Far Out life, he wanted to warn the young man. Kaph made no answer. Since he had said, "There is not enough of me left alive," he had not spoken a word.

"Owen," Martin said on suit intercom, "he's spla. Insane. Psycho."

"He's doing very well for a man who's died nine times."

"Well? Like a turned-off android is well? The only emotion he has left is hate. Look at his eyes."

"That's not hate, Martin. Listen, it's true that he has, in a sense, been dead. I cannot imagine what he feels. But it's not hatred. He can't even see us. It's too dark."

"Throats have been cut in the dark. He hates us because we're not Aleph and Yod and Zayin."

"Maybe. But I think he's alone. He doesn't see us or

hear us, that's the truth. He never had to see anyone else before. He never was alone before. He had himself to see, talk with, live with, nine other selves all his life. He doesn't know how you go it alone. He must learn. Give him time."

Martin shook his heavy head. "Spla," he said. "Just remember when you're alone with him that he could break your neck one-handed."

"He could do that," said Pugh, a short, soft-voiced man with a scarred cheekbone; he smiled. They were just outside the dome airlock, programming one of the servos to repair a damaged hauler. They could see Kaph sitting inside the great half-egg of the dome like a fly in amber.

"Hand me the insert pack there. What makes you think he'll get any better?"

"He has a strong personality, to be sure."

"Strong? Crippled. Nine-tenths dead, as he put it."

"But he's not dead. He's a live man: John Kaph Chow. He had a jolly queer upbringing, but after all every boy has got to break free of his family. He will do it."

"I can't see it."

"Think a bit, Martin bach. What's this cloning for? To repair the human race. We're in a bad way. Look at me. My IIQ and GC are half this John Chow's. Yet they wanted me so badly for the Far Out Service that when I volunteered they took me and fitted me out with an artificial lung and corrected my myopia. Now if there were enough good sound lads about would they be taking one-lunged shortsighted Welshmen?"

"Didn't know you had an artificial lung."

"I do then. Not tin, you know. Human, grown in a tank from a bit of somebody; cloned, if you like. That's how they make replacement-organs, the same general idea as cloning, but bits and pieces instead of whole people. It's my own lung now, whatever. But what I am saying is this, there are too many like me these days, and not enough like John Chow. They're trying to raise the level of the human genetic pool, which is a mucky little puddle since the population crash. So then if a man is cloned, he's a strong and clever man. It's only logic, to be sure."

Martin grunted; the servo began to hum.

Kaph had been eating little; he had trouble swallowing his food, choking on it, so that he would give up trying

75

after a few bites. He had lost eight or ten kilos. After three weeks or so, however, his appetite began to pick up, and one day he began to look through the clone's possessions, the sleeping-bags, kits, papers which Pugh had stacked neatly in a far angle of a packing-crate alley. He sorted, destroyed a heap of papers and oddments, made a small packet of what remained, then relapsed into his walking coma.

Two days later he spoke. Pugh was trying to correct a flutter in the tape-player, and failing; Martin had the jet out, checking their maps of the Pampas. "Hell and damnation!" Pugh said, and Kaph said in a toneless voice, "Do you want me to do that?"

Pugh jumped, controlled himself, and gave the machine to Kaph. The young man took it apart, put it back together, and left it on the table.

"Put on a tape," Pugh said with careful casualness, busy at another table.

Kaph put on the topmost tape, a chorale. He lay down on his cot. The sound of a hundred human voices singing together filled the dome. He lay still, his face blank.

In the next days he took over several routine jobs, unasked. He undertook nothing that wanted initiative, and if asked to do anything he made no response at all.

"He's doing well," Pugh said in the dialect of Argentina.

"He's not. He's turning himself into a machine. Does what he's programmed to do, no reaction to anything else. He's worse off than when he didn't function at all. He's not human any more."

Pugh sighed. "Well, good night," he said in English. "Good night, Kaph."

"Good night," Martin said; Kaph did not.

Next morning at breakfast Kaph reached across Martin's plate for the toast. "Why don't you ask for it," Martin said with the geniality of repressed exasperation. "I can pass it."

"I can reach it," Kaph said in his flat voice.

"Yes, but look. Asking to pass things, saying good night or hello, they're not important, but all the same when somebody says something a person ought to answer. . . ."

The young man looked indifferently in Martin's direction; his eyes still did not seem to see clear through to the person he looked toward. "Why should I answer?"

76

"Because somebody has said something to you."

"Why?"

Martin shrugged and laughed. Pugh jumped up and turned on the rock-cutter.

Later on he said, "Lay off that, please, Martin."

"Manners are essential in small isolated crews, some kind of manners, whatever you work out together. He's been taught that, everybody in Far Out knows it. Why does he deliberately flout it?"

"Do you tell yourself good night?"

"So?"

"Don't you see Kaph's never known anyone but himself?"

Martin brooded and then broke out, "Then by God this cloning business is all wrong. It won't do. What are a lot of duplicate geniuses going to do for us when they don't even know we exist?"

Pugh nodded. "It might be wiser to separate the clones and bring them up with others. But they make such a grand team this way."

"Do they? I don't know. If this lot had been ten average inefficient ET engineers, would they all have been in the same place at the same time? Would they all have got killed? What if, when the quake came and things started caving in, what if all those kids ran the same way, farther into the mine, maybe, to save the one that was farthest in? Even Kaph was outside and went in. . . . It's hypothetical. But I keep thinking, out of ten ordinary confused guys, more might have got out."

"I don't know. It's true that identical twins tend to die at about the same time, even when they have never seen each other. Identity and death, it is very strange. . . ."

The days went on, the red sun crawled across the dark sky, Kaph did not speak when spoken to, Pugh and Martin snapped at each other more frequently each day. Pugh complained of Martin's snoring. Offended, Martin moved his cot clear across the dome and also ceased speaking to Pugh for some while. Pugh whistled Welsh dirges until Martin complained, and then Pugh stopped speaking for a while.

The day before the Mission ship was due, Martin announced he was going over to Merioneth.

77

"I thought at least you'd be giving me a hand with the computer to finish the rock-analyses," Pugh said, aggrieved.

"Kaph can do that. I want one more look at the Trench. Have fun," Martin added in dialect, and laughed, and left.

"What is that language?"

"Argentinean. I told you that once, didn't I?"

"I don't know." After a while the young man added, "I have forgotten a lot of things, I think."

"It wasn't important, to be sure," Pugh said gently, realizing all at once how important this conversation was. "Will you give me a hand running the computer, Kaph?"

He nodded.

Pugh had left a lot of loose ends, and the job took them all day. Kaph was a good co-worker, quick and systematic, much more so than Pugh himself. His flat voice, now that he was talking again, got on the nerves; but it didn't matter, there was only this one day left to get through and then the ship would come, the old crew, comrades and friends.

During tea-break Kaph said, "What will happen if the Explore ship crashes?"

"They'd be killed."

"To you, I mean."

"To us? We'd radio SOS all signals, and live on half-rations till the rescue cruiser from Area Three Base came. Four and a half E-years away it is. We have life-support here for three men for, let's see, maybe between four and five years. A bit tight, it would be."

"Would they send a cruiser for three men?"

"They would."

Kaph said no more.

"Enough cheerful speculations," Pugh said cheerfully, rising to get back to work. He slipped sideways and the chair avoided his hand; he did a sort of half-pirouette and fetched up hard against the dome-hide. "My goodness," he said, reverting to his native idiom, "what is it?"

"Quake," said Kaph.

The teacups bounced on the table with a plastic cackle, a litter of papers slid off a box, the skin of the dome swelled and sagged. Underfoot there was a huge noise, half-sound half-shaking, a subsonic boom.

Kaph sat unmoved. An earthquake does not frighten a man who died in an earthquake.

Pugh, white-faced, wiry black hair sticking out, a frightened man, said, "Martin is in the Trench."

"What trench?"

"The big fault line. The epicenter for the local quakes. Look at the seismograph." Pugh struggled with the stuck door of a still-jittering locker.

"Where are you going?"

"After him."

"Martin took the jet. Sleds aren't safe to use during quakes. They go out of control."

"For God's sake, man, shut up."

Kaph stood up, speaking in a flat voice as usual. "It's unnecessary to go out after him now. It's taking an unnecessary risk."

"If his alarm goes off, radio me," Pugh said, shut the headpiece of his suit, and ran to the lock. As he went out Libra picked up her ragged skirts and danced a belly-dance from under his feet clear to the red horizon.

Inside the dome, Kaph saw the sled go up, tremble like a meteor in the dull red daylight, and vanish to the northeast. The hide of the dome quivered; the earth coughed. A vent south of the dome belched up a slow-flowing bile of black gas.

A bell shrilled and a red light flashed on the central control board. The sign under the light read Suit-Two, and scribbled under that, A.G.M. Kaph did not turn the signal off. He tried to radio Martin, then Pugh, but got no reply from either.

When the aftershocks decreased he went back to work, and finished up Pugh's job. It took him about two hours. Every half-hour he tried to contact Suit-One, and got no reply, then Suit-Two, and got no reply. The red light had stopped flashing after an hour.

It was dinnertime. Kaph cooked dinner for one, and ate it. He lay down on his cot.

The aftershocks had ceased except for faint rolling tremors at long intervals. The sun hung in the west, oblate, pale-red, immense. It did not sink visibly. There was no sound at all.

Kaph got up and began to walk about the messy, half-packed-up, overcrowded, empty dome. The silence continued. He went to the player and put on the first tape that came to hand. It was pure music, electronic, without harmonies, without voices. It ended. The silence continued.

Pugh's uniform tunic, one button missing, hung over a stack of rock-samples. Kaph stared at it a while.

The silence continued.

The child's dream: There is no one else alive in the world but me. In all the world.

Low, north of the dome, a meteor flickered.

Kaph's mouth opened as if he were trying to say something, but no sound came. He went hastily to the north wall and peered out into the gelatinous red light.

The little star came in and sank. Two figures blurred the airlock. Kaph stood close beside the lock as they came in. Martin's imsuit was covered with some kind of dust so that he looked raddled and warty like the surface of Libra. Pugh had him by the arm.

"Is he hurt?"

Pugh shucked his suit, helped Martin peel off his. "Shaken up," he said, curt.

"A piece of cliff fell onto the jet," Martin said, sitting down at the table and waving his arms. "Not while I was in it, though. I was parked, see, and poking about that carbon-dust area when I felt things humping. So I went out onto a nice bit of early igneous I'd noticed from above, good footing and out from under the cliffs. Then I saw this bit of the planet fall off onto the flyer, quite a sight it was, and after a while it occurred to me the spare aircans were in the flyer, so I leaned on the panic button. But I didn't get any radio reception, that's always happening here during quakes, so I didn't know if the signal was getting through either. And things went on jumping around and pieces of the cliff coming off. Little rocks flying around, and so dusty you couldn't see a meter ahead. I was really beginning to wonder what I'd do for breathing in the small hours, you know, when I saw old Owen buzzing up the Trench in all that dust and junk like a big ugly bat—"

"Want to eat?" said Pugh.

"Of course I want to eat. How'd you come through the quake here, Kaph? No damage? It wasn't a big one actually, was it, what's the seismo say? My trouble was I was in the middle of it. Old Epicenter Alvaro. Felt like Richter Fifteen there—total destruction of planet—"

'Sit down," Pugh said. "Eat."

After Martin had eaten a little his spate of talk ran dry. He very soon went off to his cot, still in the remote angle where he had removed it when Pugh complained of his snoring. "Good night, you one-lunged Welshman," he said across the dome.

"Good night."

There was no more out of Martin. Pugh opaqued the dome, turned the lamp down to a yellow glow less than a candle's light, and sat doing nothing, saying nothing, withdrawn.

The silence continued.

"I finished the computations."

Pugh nodded thanks.

"The signal from Martin came through, but I couldn't contact you or him."

Pugh said with effort, "I should not have gone. He had two hours of air left even with only one can. He might have been heading home when I left. This way we were all out of touch with one another. I was scared."

The silence came back, punctuated now by Martin's long, soft snores.

"Do you love Martin?"

Pugh looked up with angry eyes: "Martin is my friend. We've worked together, he's a good man." He stopped. After a while he said, "Yes, I love him. Why did you ask that?"

Kaph said nothing, but he looked at the other man. His face was changed, as if he were glimpsing something he had not seen before; his voice too was changed. "How can you . . . ? How do you . . . ?"

But Pugh could not tell him. "I don't know," he said, "it's practice, partly. I don't know. We're each of us alone, to be sure. What can you do but hold your hand out in the dark?"

Kaph's strange gaze dropped, burned out by its own intensity.

"I'm tired," Pugh said. "That was ugly, looking for him in all that black dust and muck, and mouths opening and shutting in the ground. . . . I'm going to bed. The ship will be transmitting to us by six or so." He stood up and stretched.

"It's a clone," Kaph said. "The other Exploit team they're bringing with them."

"Is it, then?"

"A twelveclone. They came out with us on the *Passerine*."

Kaph sat in the small yellow aura of the lamp seeming to look past it at what he feared: the new clone, the multiple self of which he was not part. A lost piece of a broken set, a fragment, inexpert at solitude, not knowing even how you go about giving love to another individual, now he must face the absolute, closed self-sufficiency of the clone of twelve; that was a lot to ask of the poor fellow, to be sure. Pugh put a hand on his shoulder in passing. "The chief won't ask you to stay here with a clone. You can go home. Or since you're Far Out maybe you'll come on farther out with us. We could use you. No hurry deciding. You'll make out all right."

Pugh's quiet voice trailed off. He stood unbuttoning his coat, stooped a little with fatigue. Kaph looked at him and saw the thing he had never seen before: saw him: Owen Pugh, the other, the stranger who held his hand out in the dark.

"Good night," Pugh mumbled, crawling into his sleeping-bag and half-asleep already, so that he did not hear Kaph reply after a pause, repeating, across darkness, benediction.

Since this story scrupulously avoids any explanation what-soever of its central phenomenon, it is necessarily a fantasy; the condition of possession it describes was assumed to be well-nigh as universal in the sixteenth and seventeenth centuries. Possibly it is the modern setting which makes it feel like science fiction. It embodies the only justifiable use I have ever seen of the historical present tense—to describe a people abruptly deprived of all hope of having a history.

PASSENGERS

Robert Silverberg

There are only fragments of me left now. Chunks of memory have broken free and drifted away like calved glaciers. It is always like that when a Passenger leaves us. We can never be sure of all the things our borrowed bodies did. We have only the lingering traces, the imprints.

Like sand clinging to an ocean-tossed bottle. Like the throbbings of amputated legs.

I rise. I collect myself. My hair is rumpled; I comb it. My face is creased from too little sleep. There is sourness in my mouth. Has my Passenger been eating dung with my mouth? They do that. They do anything.

It is morning.

A gray, uncertain morning. I stare at it awhile, and then, shuddering, I opaque the window and confront instead the gray, uncertain surface of the inner panel. My room looks untidy. Did I have a woman here? There are ashes in the trays. Searching for butts, I find several with lipstick stains. Yes a woman was here.

 Nebula Award, Best Short Story 1969

I touch the bedsheets. Still warm with shared warmth. Both pillows tousled. She has gone, though, and the Passenger is gone, and I am alone.

How long did it last, this time?

I pick up the phone and ring Central. "What is the date?"

The computer's bland feminine voice replies, "Friday, December fourth, nineteen eighty-seven."

"The time?"

"Nine fifty-one, Eastern Standard Time."

"The weather forecast?"

"Predicted temperature, thirty-one. Wind from the north, sixteen miles an hour. Chances of precipitation slight."

"What do you recommend for a hangover?"

"Food or medication?"

"Anything you like," I say.

The computer mulls that one over for a while. Then it decides on both, and activates my kitchen. The spigot yields cold tomato juice. Eggs begin to fry. From the medicine slot comes a purplish liquid. The Central Computer is always so thoughtful. Do the Passengers ever ride it, I wonder? What thrills could that hold for them? Surely it must be more exciting to borrow the million minds of Central than to live a while in the faulty short-circuited soul of a corroding human being!

December 4, Central said. Friday. So the Passenger had me for three nights.

I drink the purplish stuff and probe my memories in a gingerly way, as one might probe a festering sore.

I remember Tuesday morning. A bad time at work. None of the charts will come out right. The section manager irritable; he has been taken by Passengers three times in five weeks, and his section is in disarray as a result, and his Christmas bonus is jeopardized. Even though it is customary not to penalize a person for lapses due to Passengers, according to the system, the section manager seems to feel he will be treated unfairly. So he treats us unfairly. We have a hard time. Revise the charts, fiddle with the program, check the fundamentals ten times over. Out they come: the detailed forecasts for price variations of public utility securities, February—April 1988. That afternoon we are to meet and discuss the charts and what they tell us.

I do not remember Tuesday afternoon.

That must have been when the Passenger took me. Perhaps at work; perhaps in the mahogany-paneled board-room itself, during the conference. Pink concerned faces all about me; I cough, I lurch, I stumble from my seat. They shake their heads sadly. No one reaches for me. No one stops me. It is too dangerous to interfere with one who has a Passenger. The chances are great that a second Passenger lurks nearby in the discorporate state looking for a mount. So I am avoided. I leave the building.

After that, what?

Sitting in my room on bleak Friday morning, I eat my scrambled eggs and try to reconstruct the three lost nights.

Of course it is impossible. The conscious mind functions during the period of captivity, but upon withdrawal of the Passenger nearly every recollection goes too. There is only a slight residue, a gritty film of faint and ghostly memories. The mount is never precisely the same person afterwards; though he cannot recall the details of his experience, he is subtly changed by it.

I try to recall.

A girl? Yes: lipstick on the butts. Sex, then, here in my room. Young? Old? Blonde? Dark? Everything is hazy. How did my borrowed body behave? Was I a good lover? I try to be, when I am myself. I keep in shape. At 38, I can handle three sets of tennis on a summer afternoon without collapsing. I can make a woman glow as a woman is meant to glow. Not boasting: just categorizing. We have our skills. These are mine.

But Passengers, I am told, take wry amusement in controverting our skills. So would it have given my rider a kind of delight to find me a woman and force me to fail repeatedly with her?

I dislike that thought.

The fog is going from my mind now. The medicine prescribed by Central works rapidly. I eat, I shave, I stand under the vibrator until my skin is clean. I do my exercises. Did the Passenger exercise my body Wednesday and Thursday morning? Probably not. I must make up for that. I am close to middle age, now; tonus lost is not easily regained.

I touch my toes twenty times, knees stiff.

I kick my legs in the air.

85

I lie flat and lift myself on pumping elbows.

Th body responds, maltreated though it has been. It is the first bright moment of my awakening: to feel the inner tingling, to know that I still have vigor.

Fresh air is what I want next. Quickly I slip into my clothes and leave. There is no need for me to report to work today. They are aware that since Tuesday afternoon I have had a Passenger; they need not be aware that before dawn on Friday the Passenger departed. I will have a free day. I will walk the city's streets, stretching my limbs, repaying my body for the abuse it has suffered.

I enter the elevator. I drop fifty stories to the ground. I step out into the December dreariness.

The towers of New York rise about me.

In the street the cars stream forward. Drivers sit edgily at their wheels. One never knows when the driver of a nearby car will be borrowed, and there is always a moment of lapsed coordination as the Passenger takes over. Many lives are lost that way on our streets and highways; but never the life of a Passenger.

I begin to walk without purpose. I cross Fourteenth Street, heading north, listening to the soft violent purr of the electric engines. I see a boy jigging in the street and know he is being ridden. At Fifth and Twenty-second a prosperous-looking paunchy man approaches, his necktie askew, this morning's *Wall Street Journal* jutting from an overcoat pocket. He giggles. He thrusts out his tongue. Ridden. Ridden. I avoid him. Moving briskly, I come to the underpass that carries traffic below Thirty-fourth Street toward Queens, and pause for a moment to watch two adolescent girls quarreling at the rim of the pedestrian walk. One is a Negro. Her eyes are rolling in terror. The other pushes her closer to the railing. Ridden. But the Passenger does not have murder on its mind, merely pleasure. The Negro girl is released and falls in a huddled heap, trembling. Then she rises and runs. The other girl draws a long strand of gleaming hair into her mouth, chews on it, seems to awaken. She looks dazed.

I avert my eyes. One does not watch while a fellow sufferer is awakening. There is a morality of the ridden; we have so many new tribal mores in these dark days.

I hurry on.

Where am I going so hurriedly? Already I have walked

more than a mile. I seem to be moving toward some goal, as though my Passenger still hunches in my skull, urging me about. But I know that is not so. For the moment, at least, I am free.

Can I be sure of that?

Cogito ergo sum no longer applies. We go on thinking even while we are ridden, and we live in quiet desperation, unable to halt our courses no matter how ghastly, no matter how self-destructive. I am certain that I can distinguish between the condition of bearing a Passenger and the condition of being free. But perhaps not. Perhaps I bear a particularly devilish Passenger which has not quitted me at all, but which merely has receded to the cerebellum, leaving me the illusion of freedom while all the time surreptitiously driving me onward to some purpose of its own.

Did we ever have more than that: the illusion of freedom?

But this is disturbing, the thought that I may be ridden without realizing it. I burst out in heavy perspiration, not merely from the exertion of walking. Stop. Stop here. Why must you walk? You are at Forty-second Street. There is the library. Nothing forces you onward. Stop a while, I tell myself. Rest on the library steps.

I sit on the cold stone and tell myself that I have made this decision for myself.

Have I? It is the old problem, free will versus determinism, translated into the foulest of forms. Determinism is no longer a philosopher's abstraction; it is cold alien tendrils sliding between the cranial sutures. The Passengers arrived three years ago. I have been ridden five times since then. Our world is quite different now. But we have adjusted even to this. We have adjusted. We have our mores. Life goes on. Our governments rule, our legislatures meet, our stock exchanges transact business as usual, and we have methods for compensating for the random havoc. It is the only way. What else can we do? Shrivel in defeat? We have an enemy we cannot fight; at best we can resist through endurance. So we endure.

The stone steps are cold against my body. In December few people sit here.

I tell myself that I made this long walk of my own free will, that I halted of my own free will, that no Passenger rides my brain now. Perhaps. Perhaps. I cannot let myself believe that I am not free.

Can it be, I wonder, that the Passenger left some lingering command in me? Walk to this place, halt at this place? That is possible too.

I look about me at the others on the library steps.

An old man, eyes vacant, sitting on newspaper. A boy of thirteen or so with flaring nostrils. A plump woman. Are all of them ridden? Passengers seem to cluster about me today. The more I study the ridden ones, the more convinced I become that I am, for the moment, free. The last time, I had three months of freedom between rides. Some people, they say, are scarcely ever free. Their bodies are in great demand, and they know only scattered bursts of freedom, a day here, a week there, an hour. We have never been able to determine how many Passengers infest our world. Millions, maybe. Or maybe five. Who can tell?

A wisp of snow curls down out of the gray sky. Central had said the chance of precipitation was slight. Are they riding Central this morning too?

I see the girl.

She sits diagonally across from me, five steps up and a hundred feet away, her black skirt pulled up on her knees to reveal handsome legs. She is young. Her hair is deep, rich auburn. Her eyes are pale; at this distance, I cannot make out the precise color. She is dressed simply. She is younger than thirty. She wears a dark green coat and her lipstick has a purplish tinge. Her lips are full, her nose slender, high-bridged, her eyebrows carefully plucked.

I know her.

I have spent the past three nights with her in my room. She is the one. Ridden, she came to me, and ridden, I slept with her. I am certain of this. The veil of memory opens, I see her slim body naked on my bed.

How can it be that I remember this?

It is too strong to be an illusion. Clearly this is something that I have been *permitted* to remember for reasons I cannot comprehend. And I remember more. I remember her soft gasping sounds of pleasure. I know that my own body did not betray me those three nights, nor did I fail her need.

And there is more. A memory of sinuous music; a scent

88

How do your cigarette's tar and nicotine numbers compare with True?

LATEST U.S. GOVERNMENT TESTS:
13 MGS. TAR. 0.7 MGS. NICOTINE

Place your pack here.

Compare
your cigarette's
tar and nicotine
numbers
with True.

LATEST U.S. GOVERNMENT TESTS:
12 MGS. TAR. 0.6 MGS. NICOTINE

No numbers on the front of your pack? True puts its numbers right out front. Because True, regular and menthol, is lower in both tar and nicotine than 99% of all other cigarettes sold. Think about it.

LATEST U.S. GOVERNMENT TESTS:
12 MGS. TAR, 0.6 MGS. NICOTINE

© Lorillard 1971

20 CLASS A CIGARETTES

TRUE
FILTER CIGARETTES

Warning: The Surgeon General Has Determined That Cigarette Smoking Is Dangerous to Your Health

Regular or menthol.
Doesn't it all add up to True?

Regular: 12 mg. "tar", 0.6 mg. nicotine,
Menthol: 13 mg. "tar", 0.7 mg. nicotine, av. per cigarette, FTC Report, Aug. '71.

of youth in her hair; the rustle of winter trees. Somehow she brings back to me a time of innocence, a time when I am young and girls are mysterious, a time of parties and dances and warmth and secrets.

I am drawn to her now.

There is an etiquette about such things, too. It is in poor taste to approach someone you have met while being ridden. Such an encounter gives you no privilege; a stranger remains a stranger, no matter what you and she may have done and said during your involuntary time together.

Yet I am drawn to her.

Why this violation of taboo? Why this raw breach of etiquette? I have never done this before. I have been scrupulous.

But I get to my feet and walk along the step on which I have been sitting, until I am below her, and I look up, and automatically she folds her ankles together and angles her knees as if in awareness that her position is not a modest one. I know from that gesture that she is not ridden now. My eyes meet hers. Her eyes are hazy green. She is beautiful, and I rack my memory for more details of our passion.

I climb step by step until I stand before her.

"Hello," I say.

She gives me a neutral look. She does not seem to recognize me. Her eyes are veiled, as one's eyes often are, just after the Passenger has gone. She purses her lips and appraises me in a distant way.

"Hello," she replies coolly. "I don't think I know you."

"No. You don't. But I have the feeling you don't want to be alone just now. And I know I don't." I try to persuade her with my eyes that my motives are decent. "There's snow in the air," I say. "We can find a warmer place. I'd like to talk to you."

"About what?"

"Let's go elsewhere, and I'll tell you. I'm Charles Roth."

"Helen Martin."

She gets to her feet. She still has not cast aside her cool neutrality; she is suspicious, ill at ease. But at least she is willing to go with me. A good sign.

"Is it too early in the day for a drink?" I ask.

"I'm not sure. I hardly know what time it is."

"Before noon."

"Let's have a drink anyway," she says, and we both smile.

We go to a cocktail lounge across the street. Sitting face to face in the darkness, we sip drinks, daiquiri for her, bloody mary for me. She relaxes a little. I ask myself what it is I want from her. The pleasure of her company, yes. Her company in bed? But I have already had that pleasure, three nights of it, though she does not know that. I want something more. Something more. What?

Her eyes are bloodshot. She has had little sleep these past three nights.

I say, "Was it very unpleasant for you?"

"What?"

"The Passenger."

A whiplash of reaction crosses her face. "How did you know I've had a Passenger?"

"I know."

"We aren't supposed to talk about it."

"I'm broadminded," I tell her. "My Passenger left me some time during the night. I was ridden since Tuesday afternoon."

"Mine left me about two hours ago, I think." Her cheeks color. She is doing something daring, talking like this. "I was ridden since Monday night. This was my fifth time."

"Mine also."

We toy with our drinks. Rapport is growing, almost without the need of words. Our recent experiences with Passengers give us something in common, although Helen does not realize how intimately we shared those experiences.

We talk. She is a designer of display windows. She has a small apartment several blocks from here. She lives alone. She asks me what I do. "Securities analyst," I tell her. She smiles. Her teeth are flawless. We have a second round of drinks. I am positive, now, that this is the girl who was in my room while I was ridden.

A seed of hope grows in me. It was a happy chance that brought us together again, so soon after we parted as dreamers. A happy chance, too, that some vestige of the dream lingered in my mind.

We have shared something, who knows what, and it must have been good to leave such a vivid imprint on me, and now I want to come to her conscious, aware, my own master, and renew that relationship, making it a real one this time. It is not proper, for I am trespassing on a privilege that is not mine except by virtue of our Passengers' brief presence in us. Yet I need her. I want her.

She seems to need me, too, without realizing who I am. But fear holds her back.

I am frightened of frightening her, and I do not try to press my advantage too quickly. Perhaps she would take me to her apartment with her now, perhaps not, but I do not ask. We finish our drinks. We arrange to meet by the library steps again tomorrow. My hand momentarily brushes hers. Then she is gone.

I fill three ashtrays that night. Over and over I debate the wisdom of what I am doing. But why not leave her alone? I have no right to follow her. In the place our world has become, we are wisest to remain apart.

And yet—there is that stab of half-memory when I think of her. The blurred lights of lost chances behind the stairs, of girlish laughter in second-floor corridors, of stolen kisses, of tea and cake. I remember the girl with the orchid in her hair, and the one in the spangled dress, and the one with the child's face and the woman's eyes, all so long ago, all lost, all gone, and I tell myself that this one I will not lose, I will not permit her to be taken from me.

Morning comes, a quiet Saturday. I return to the library, hardly expecting to find her there, but she is there, on the steps, and the sight of her is like a reprieve. She looks wary, troubled; obviously she has done much thinking, little sleeping. Together we walk along Fifth Avenue. She is quite close to me, but she does not take my arm. Her steps are brisk, short, nervous.

I want to suggest that we go to her apartment instead of to the cocktail lounge. In these days we must move swiftly while we are free. But I know it would be a mistake to think of this as a matter of tactics. Coarse haste would be fatal, bringing me perhaps an ordinary victory, a numbing defeat within it. In any event her mood hardly seems promising. I look at her, thinking of string music and new snowfalls, and she looks toward the gray sky.

She says, "I can feel them watching me all the time.

Like vultures swooping overhead, waiting, waiting. Ready to pounce."

"But there's a way of beating them. We can grab little scraps of life when they're not looking."

"They're *always* looking."

"No," I tell her. "There can't be enough of them for that. Sometimes they're looking the other way. And while they are, two people can come together and try to share warmth."

"But what's the use?"

"You're too pessimistic, Helen. They ignore us for months at a time. We have a chance. We have a chance."

But I cannot break through her shell of fear. She is paralyzed by the nearness of the Passengers, unwilling to begin anything for fear it will be snatched away by our tormentors. We reach the building where she lives, and I hope she will relent and invite me in. For an instant she wavers, but only for an instant: she takes my hand in both of hers, and smiles, and the smile fades, and she is gone, leaving me only with the words, "Let's meet at the library again tomorrow. Noon."

I make the long chilling walk home alone.

Some of her pessimism seeps into me that night. It seems futile for us to try to salvage anything. More than that: wicked for me to seek her out, shameful to offer a hesitant love when I am not free. In this world, I tell myself, we should keep well clear of others, so that we do not harm anyone when we are seized and ridden.

I do not go to meet her in the morning.

It is best this way, I insist, I have no business trifling with her. I imagine her at the library, wondering why I am late, growing tense, impatient, then annoyed. She will be angry with me for breaking our date, but her anger will ebb, and she will forget me quickly enough.

Monday comes. I return to work.

Naturally, no one discusses my absence. It is as though I have never been away. The market is strong that morning. The work is challenging; it is mid-morning before I think of Helen at all. But once I think of her, I can think of nothing else. My cowardice in standing her up. The childishness of Saturday night's dark thoughts. Why accept fate so passively? Why give in? I want to fight, now, to carve out a pocket of security despite the odds. I feel a deep conviction that it can be done. The Passengers may never bother the two of us again, after all. And that flickering smile of hers outside her building Saturday, that momentary glow—it should have told me that behind her wall of fear she felt the same hopes. She was waiting for me to lead the way. And I stayed home instead.

At lunchtime I go to the library, convinced it is futile. But she is there. She paces along the steps; the wind slices at her slender figure. I go to her.

She is silent a moment. "Hello," she says finally.

"I'm sorry about yesterday."

"I waited a long time for you."

I shrug. "I made up my mind that it was no use to come. But then I changed my mind again."

She tries to look angry. But I know she is pleased to see me again—else why did she come here today? She cannot hide her inner pleasure. Nor can I. I point across the street to the cocktail lounge.

"A daiquiri?" I say. "As a peace offering?"

"All right."

Today the lounge is crowded, but we find a booth somehow. There is a brightness in her eyes that I have not seen before. I sense that a barrier is crumbling within her.

"You're less afraid of me, Helen," I say.

"I've never been afraid of you. I'm afraid of what could happen if we take the risks."

"Don't be. Don't be."

"I'm trying not to be afraid. But sometimes it seems so hopeless. Since *they* came here—"

"We can still try to live our own lives."

"Maybe."

"We have to. Let's make a pact, Helen. No more gloom. No more worrying about the terrible things that might just maybe happen. All right?"

A pause. Then a cool hand against mine.

"All right."

We finish our drinks, and I present my Credit Central to pay for them, and we go outside. I want her to tell me to forget about this afternoon's work and come home with her. It is inevitable, now, that she will ask me, and better sooner than later.

We walk a block. She does not offer the invitation. I

sense the struggle inside her, and I wait, letting that struggle reach its own resolution without interference from me. We walk a second block. Her arm is through mine, but she talks only of her work, of the weather, and it is a remote, arm's-length conversation. At the next corner she swings around, away from her apartment, back toward the cocktail lounge. I try to be patient with her.

I have no need to rush things now, I tell myself. Her body is not a secret to me. We have begun our relationship topsy-turvy, with the physical part first; now it will take time to work backward to the more difficult part that some people call love.

But of course she is not aware that we have known each other that way. The wind blows swirling snowflakes in our faces, and somehow the cold sting awakens honesty in me. I know what I must say. I must relinquish my unfair advantage.

I tell her, "While I was ridden last week, Helen, I had a girl in my room."

"Why talk of such things now?"

"I have to, Helen. You were the girl."

She halts. She turns to me. People hurry past us in the street. Her face is very pale, with dark red spots growing in her cheeks.

"That's not funny, Charles."

"It wasn't meant to be. You were with me from Tuesday night to early Friday morning."

"How can you possibly know that?"

"I do. I do. The memory is clear. Somehow it remains, Helen. I see your whole body."

"Stop it, Charles."

"We were very good together," I say. "We must have pleased our Passengers because we were so good. To see you again—it was like waking from a dream, and finding that the dream was real, the girl right there—"

"No!"

"Let's go to your apartment and begin again."

She says, "You're being deliberately filthy, and I don't know why, but there wasn't any reason for you to spoil things. Maybe I was with you and maybe I wasn't, but you wouldn't know it, and if you did know it you should keep your mouth shut about it, and—"

94

"You have a birthmark the size of a dime," I say, "about three inches below your left breast."

She sobs and hurls herself at me, there in the street. Her long silvery nails assail me. No one pays attention; those who pass by assume we are ridden, and turn their heads. She is all fury, but I have my arms around hers like metal bands, so that she can only stamp and snort, and her body is close against mine. She is rigid, anguished.

In a low, urgent voice I say, "We'll defeat them, Helen. We'll finish what they started. Don't fight me. There's no reason to fight me. I know, it's a fluke that I remember you, but let me go with you and I'll prove that we belong together."

"Let—go—"

"Please. Please. Why should we be enemies? I don't mean you any harm. I love you, Helen. Do you remember, when we were kids, we could play at being in love? I did; you must have done it too. Sixteen, seventeen years old. The whispers, the conspiracies—all a big game, and we knew it. But the game's over. We can't afford to tease and run. We have so little time, when we're free—we have to trust, to open ourselves—"

"It's wrong."

"No. Just because it's the stupid custom for two people brought together by Passengers to avoid one another, that doesn't mean we have to follow it. Helen—Helen—"

Something in my tone registers with her. She ceases to struggle. Her rigid body softens. She looks up at me, her tearstreaked face thawing, her eyes blurred.

"Trust me," I say. "Trust me, Helen!"

She hesitates. Then she smiles.

In that moment I feel the chill at the back of my skull, the sensation as of a steel needle driven deep through bone. I stiffen. My arms drop away from her. For an instant, I lose touch, and when the mists clear all is different.

"Charles?" she says. *"Charles?"*

Her knuckles are against her teeth. I turn, ignoring her, and go back into the cocktail lounge. A young man sits in one of the front booths. His dark hair gleams with pomade; his cheeks are smooth. His eyes meet mine.

I sit down. He orders drinks. We do not talk.

95

My hand falls on his wrist, and remains there. The bartender, serving the drinks, scowls but says nothing. We sip our cocktails and put the drained glasses down.

"Let's go," the young man says.

I follow him out.

Larry Niven has said that he writes plotty, technologically oriented science fiction—which has already won him a "Hugo" award—because he feels that his writing is weak on atmosphere and characterization. This muted, rather Cabell-like parable, another pure fantasy, is thus something of a sport; but the SFWA voting suggests that it shows a facet of his talent which, perhaps, he ought to reevaluate.

NOT LONG BEFORE THE END

Larry Niven

A swordsman battled a sorcerer, once upon a time.

In that age such battles were frequent. A natural antipathy exists between swordsmen and sorcerers, as between cats and small birds, or between rats and men. Usually the swordsman lost, and humanity's average intelligence rose some trifling fraction. Sometimes the swordsman won, and again the species was improved; for a sorcerer who cannot kill one miserable swordsman is a poor excuse for a sorcerer.

But this battle differed from the others. On one side, the sword itself was enchanted. On the other, the sorcerer knew a great and terrible truth.

We will call him the Warlock, as his name is both forgotten and impossible to pronounce. His parents had known what they were about. He who knows your name has power over you, but he must speak your name to use it.

The Warlock had found his terrible truth in middle age.

By that time he had traveled widely. It was not from choice. It was simply that he was a powerful magician, and he used his power, and he needed friends.

He knew spells to make people love a magician. The Warlock had tried these, but he did not like the side effects. So he commonly used his great power to help those around him, that they might love him without coercion.

He found that when he had been ten to fifteen years in a place, using his magic as whim dictated, his powers would weaken. If he moved away, they returned. Twice he had had to move, and twice he had settled in a new land, learned new customs, made new friends. It happened a third time, and he prepared to move again. But something set him to wondering.

Why should a man's powers be so unfairly drained out of him?

It happened to nations too. Throughout history, those lands which had been richest in magic had been overrun by barbarians carrying swords and clubs. It was a sad truth, and one that did not bear thinking about, but the Warlock's curiosity was strong.

So he wondered, and he stayed to perform certain experiments.

His last experiment involved a simple kinetic sorcery set to spin a metal disc in midair. And when that magic was done, he knew a truth he could never forget.

So he departed. In succeeding decades he moved again and again. Time changed his personality, if not his body, and his magic became more dependable, if less showy. He had discovered a great and terrible truth, and if he kept it secret, it was through compassion. His truth spelled the end of civilization, yet it was of no earthly use to anyone.

So he thought. But some five decades later (the date was on the order of 12,000 B.C.) it occurred to him that all truths find a use somewhere, sometime. And so he built another disc and recited spells over it, so that (like a telephone number already dialed but for one digit) the disc would be ready if ever he needed it.

The name of the sword was Glirendree. It was several hundred years old, and quite famous.

As for the swordsman, his name is no secret. It was

Belhap Sattlestone Wirldess ag Miracloat roo Cononson. His friends, who tended to be temporary, called him Hap. He was a barbarian, of course. A civilized man would have had more sense than to touch Glirendree, and better morals than to stab a sleeping woman. Which was how Hap had acquired his sword. Or vice versa.

The Warlock recognized it long before he saw it. He was at work in the cavern he had carved beneath a hill, when an alarm went off. The hair rose up, tingling, along the back of his neck. "Visitors," he said.

"I don't hear anything," said Sharla, but there was an uneasiness to her tone. Sharla was a girl of the village who had come to live with the Warlock. That day she had persuaded the Warlock to teach her some of his simpler spells.

"Don't you feel the hair rising on the back of your neck? I set the alarm to do that. Let me just check . . ." He used a sensor like a silver hula hoop set on edge. "There's trouble coming. Sharla, we've got to get you out of here."

"But . . ." Sharla waved protestingly at the table where they had been working.

"Oh, that. We can quit in the middle. That spell isn't dangerous." It was a charm against lovespells, rather messy to work, but safe and tame and effective. The Warlock pointed at the spear of light glaring through the hoopsensor. "That's dangerous. An enormously powerful focus of mana power is moving up the west side of the hill. You go down the east side."

"Can I help? You've taught me *some* magic."

The magician laughed a little nervously. "Against that? That's Glirendree. Look at the size of the image, the color, the shape. No. You get out of here, and right now. The hill's clear on the eastern slope."

"Come with me."

"I can't. Not with Glirendree loose. Not when it's already got hold of some idiot. There are obligations."

They came out of the cavern together, into the mansion they shared. Sharla, still protesting, donned robe and started down the hill. The Warlock hastily selected an armload of paraphernalia and went outside.

The intruder was halfway up the hill: a large but apparently human being carrying something long and glittering. He was still a quarter of an hour downslope. The Warlock set up the silver hula hoop and looked through it.

The sword was a flame of mana discharge, an eye-hurting needle of white light. Glirendree, right enough. He knew of other, equally powerful mana foci, but none were portable, and none would show as a sword to the unaided eye.

He should have told Sharla to inform the Brotherhood. She had that much magic. Too late now.

There was no colored borderline to the spear of light.

No green fringe effect meant no protective spells. The swordsman had not tried to guard himself against what he carried. Certainly the intruder was no magician, and he had not the intelligence to get the help of a magician. Did he know *nothing* about Glirendree?

Not that that would help the Warlock. He who carries Glirendree was invulnerable to any power save Glirendree itself. Or so it was said.

"Let's test that," said the Warlock to himself. He dipped into his armload of equipment and came up with something wooden, shaped like an ocarina. He blew the dust off it, raised it in his fist and pointed it down the mountain. But he hesitated.

The loyalty spell was simple and safe, but it did have side effects. It lowered its victim's intelligence.

"Self-defense," the Warlock reminded himself, and blew into the ocarina.

The swordsman did not break stride. Glirendree didn't even glow; it had absorbed the spell that easily.

In minutes the swordsman would be here. The Warlock hurriedly set up a simple prognostics spell. At least he could learn who would win the coming battle.

No picture formed before him. The scenery did not even waver.

"Well now," said the Warlock. "*Well,* now!" And he reached into his clutter of sorcerous tools and found a metal disc. Another instant's rummaging produced a double-edged knife, profusely inscribed in no known language, and very sharp.

At the top of the Warlock's hill was a spring, and the stream from that spring ran past the Warlock's house.

The swordsman stood leaning on his sword, facing the Warlock across that stream. He breathed deeply, for it had been a hard climb.

He was powerfully muscled and profusely scarred. To the Warlock it seemed strange that so young a man should have found time to acquire so many scars. But none of his wounds had impaired motor functions. The Warlock had watched him coming up the hill. The swordsman was in top physical shape.

His eyes were deep blue and brilliant, and half an inch too close together for the Warlock's taste.

"I am Hap," he called across the stream. "Where is she?"

"You mean Sharla, of course. But why is that your concern?"

"I have come to free her from her shameful bondage, old man. Too long have you—"

"Hey, hey, hey. Sharla's my *wife*."

"Too long have you used her for your vile and lecherous purposes. Too—"

"She stays of her own free will, you nit!"

"You expect me to believe that? As lovely a woman as Sharla, could she love an old and feeble warlock?"

"Do I look feeble?"

The Warlock did not look like an old man. He seemed Hap's age, some twenty years old, and his frame and his musculature were the equal of Hap's. He had not bothered to dress as he left the cavern. In place of Hap's scars, his back bore a tattoo in red and green and gold, an elaborately curlicued pentagramic design, almost hypnotic in its extradimensional involutions.

"Everyone in the village knows your age," said Hap. "You're two hundred years old, if not more."

"Hap," said the Warlock. "Belhap Something-or-other roo Cononson. Now I remember. Sharla told me you tried to bother her last time she went to the village. I should have done something about it then."

"Old man, you lie. Sharla is under a spell. Everybody knows the power of a Warlock's loyalty spell."

"I don't use them. I don't like the side effects. Who wants to be surrounded by friendly morons?" The Warlock pointed to Glirendree. "Do you know what you carry?"

Hap nodded ominously.

"Then you ought to know better. Maybe it's not too late. See if you can transfer it to your left hand."

"I tried that. I can't let go of it." Hap cut at the air, restlessly, with his sixty pounds of sword. "I have to sleep with the damned thing clutched in my hand."

"Well, it's too late then."

"It's worth it," Hap said grimly. "For now I can kill you. Too long has an innocent woman been subjected to your lecherous—"

"I know, I know." The Warlock changed languages suddenly, speaking high and fast. He spoke thus for almost a minute, then switched back to Rynaldese. "Do you feel any pain?"

"Not a twinge," said Hap. He had not moved. He stood with his remarkable sword at the ready, glowering at the magician across the stream.

"No sudden urge to travel? Attacks of remorse? Change of body temperature?" But Hap was grinning now, not at all nicely. "I thought not. Well, it had to be tried."

There was an instant of blinding light.

When it reached the vicinity of the hill, the meteorite had dwindled to the size of a baseball. It should have finished its journey at the back of Hap's head. Instead, it exploded a millisecond too soon. When the light had died, Hap stood within a ring of craterlets.

The swordsman's unsymmetrical jaw dropped, and then he closed his mouth and started forward. The sword hummed faintly.

The Warlock turned his back.

Hap curled his lip at the Warlock's cowardice. Then he jumped three feet backward from a standing start. A shadow had pulled itself from the Warlock's back.

In a lunar cave with the sun glaring into its mouth, a man's shadow on the wall might have looked that sharp and black. The shadow dropped to the ground and stood up, a humanoid outline that was less a shape than a window view of the ultimate blackness beyond the death of the universe. Then it leapt.

Glirendree seemed to move of its own accord. It hacked the demon once lengthwise and once across, while the demon seemed to batter against an invisible shield, trying to reach Hap even as it died.

102

"Clever," Hap panted. "A pentagram on your back, a demon trapped inside."

"That's clever," said the Warlock, "but it didn't work. Carrying Glirendree works, but it's not clever. I ask you again, do you know what you carry?"

"The most powerful sword ever forged." Hap raised the weapon high. His right arm was more heavily muscled than his left, and inches longer, as if Glirendree had been at work on it. "A sword to make me the equal of any warlock or sorceress, and without the help of demons, either. I had to kill a woman who loved me to get it, but I paid that price gladly. When I have sent you to your just reward, Sharla will come to me—"

"She'll spit in your eye. Now will you listen to me? Glirendree *is* a demon. If you had an ounce of sense, you'd cut your arm off at the elbow."

Hap looked startled. "You mean there's a demon imprisoned in the metal?"

"Get it through your head. *There is no metal.* It's a demon, a bound demon, and it's a parasite. It'll age you to death in a year unless you cut it loose. A Warlock of the northlands imprisoned it in its present form, then gave it to one of his bastards, Jeery of Something-or-other. Jeery conquered half this continent before he died on the battlefield, of senile decay. It was given into the charge of the Rainbow Witch a year before I was born, because there never was a woman who had less use for people, especially men."

"Probably Glirendree's doing. Started her glands up again, did it? She should have guarded against that."

"A year," said Hap. "One year."

But the sword stirred restlessly in his hand. "It will be a glorious year," said Hap, and he came forward.

The Warlock picked up a copper disc. "Four," he said, and the disc spun in midair.

By the time Hap had sloshed through the stream, the disc was a blur of motion. The Warlock moved to keep it between himself and Hap, and Hap dared not touch it, for it would have sheared through anything at all. He crossed around it, but again the Warlock had darted to the other side. In the pause he snatched up something else: a silvery knife, profusely inscribed.

"Whatever that is," said Hap, "it can't hurt me. No magic can affect me while I carry Glirendree."

"True enough," said the Warlock. "The disc will lose its force in a minute anyway. In the meantime, I know a secret that I would like to tell, one I could never tell to a friend."

Hap raised Glirendree above his head and, two-handed, swung it down on the disc. The sword stopped jarringly at the disc's rim.

"It's protecting you," said the Warlock. "If Glirendree hit the rim now, the recoil would knock you clear down to the village. Can't you hear the hum?"

Hap heard the whine as the disc cut the air. The tone was going up and up the scale.

"You're stalling," he said.

"That's true. So? Can it hurt you?"

"No. You were saying you knew a secret." Hap braced himself, sword raised, on one side of the disc, which now glowed red at the edge.

"I've wanted to tell someone for such a long time. A hundred and fifty years. Even Sharla doesn't know." The Warlock still stood ready to run if the swordsman should come after him. "I'd learned a little magic in those days, not much compared to what I know now, but big, showy stuff. Castles floating in the air. Dragons with golden scales. Armies turned to stone, or wiped out by lightning, instead of simple death spells. Stuff like that takes a lot of power, you know."

"I've heard of such things."

"I did it all the time, for myself, for friends, for whoever happened to be king, or whomever I happened to be in love with. And I found that after I'd been settled for a while, the power would leave me. I'd have to move elsewhere to get it back."

The copper disc glowed bright orange with the heat of its spin. It should have fragmented, or melted, long ago.

"Then there are the dead places, the places where a warlock dares not go. Places where magic doesn't work. They tend to be rural areas, farmlands and sheep ranges, you can find the old cities, the castles built to float which now lie tilted on their sides, the unnaturally aged bones of dragons, like huge lizards from another age.

104

"So I started wondering."

Hap stepped back a bit from the heat of the disc. It glowed pure white now, and it was like a sun brought to earth. Through the glare Hap had lost sight of the Warlock.

"So I built a disc like this one and set it spinning. Just a simple kinetic sorcery, but with a constant acceleration and no limit point. You know what mana is?"

"What's happening to your voice?"

"Mana is the name we give to the power behind magic." The Warlock's voice had gone weak and high.

A horrible suspicion came to Hap. The Warlock had slipped down the hill, leaving his voice behind! Hap trotted around the disc, shading his eyes from its heat.

An old man sat on the other side of the disc. His arthritic fingers, half-crippled with swollen joints, played with a runeinscribed knife. "What I found out—oh, there you are. Well, it's too late now."

Hap raised his sword, and his sword changed.

It was a massive red demon, horned and hooved, and its teeth were in Hap's right hand. It paused, deliberately, for the few seconds it took Hap to realize what had happened and to try to jerk away. Then it bit down, and the swordsman's hand was off at the wrist.

The demon reached out, slowly enough, but Hap in his surprise was unable to move. He felt the taloned fingers close his windpipe.

He felt the strength leak out of the taloned hand, and he saw surprise and dismay spread across the demon's face.

The disc exploded. All at once and nothing first, it disintegrated into a flat cloud of metallic particles and was gone, flashing away as so much meteorite dust. The light was as lightning striking at one's feet. The sound was its thunder. The smell was vaporized copper.

The demon faded, as a chameleon fades against its background. Fading, the demon slumped to the ground in slow motion, and faded further, and was gone. When Hap reached out with his foot, he touched only dirt.

Behind Hap was a trench of burnt earth.

The spring had stopped. The rocky bottom of the stream was drying in the sun.

The Warlock's cavern had collapsed. The furnishings

of the Warlock's mansion had gone crashing down into that vast pit, but the mansion itself was gone without trace.

Hap clutched his messily severed wrist, and he said, "But what happened?"

"Mana," the Warlock mumbled. He spat out a complete set of blackened teeth. "Mana. What I discovered was that the power behind magic is a natural resource, like the fertility of the soil. When you use it up, it's gone."

"But—"

"Can you see why I kept it a secret? One day all the wide world's mana will be used up. No more mana, no more magic. Do you know that Atlantis is tectonically unstable? Succeeding sorcerer-kings renew the spells each generation to keep the whole continent from sliding into the sea. What happens when the spells don't work any more? They couldn't possibly evacuate the whole continent in time. Kinder not to let them know."

"But . . . that disc."

The Warlock grinned with his empty mouth and ran his hands through snowy hair. All the hair came off in his fingers, leaving his scalp bare and mottled. "Senility is like being drunk. The disc? I told you. A kinetic sorcery with no upper limit. The disc keeps accelerating until all the mana in the locality has been used up."

Hap moved a step forward. Shock had drained half his strength. His foot came down jarringly, as if all the spring were out of his muscles.

"You tried to kill me."

The Warlock nodded. "I figured if the disc didn't explode and kill you while you were trying to go around it, Glirendree would strangle you when the constraint wore off. What are you complaining about? It cost you a hand, but you're free of Glirendree."

Hap took another step, and another. His hand was beginning to hurt, and the pain gave him strength. "Old man," he said thickly. "Two hundred years old. I can break your neck with the hand you left me. And I will."

The Warlock raised the inscribed knife.

"That won't work. No more magic." Hap slapped the Warlock's hand away and took the Warlock by his bony throat.

The Warlock's hand brushed easily aside, and came

106

back, and up. Hap wrapped his arms around his belly and backed away with his eyes and mouth wide open. He sat down hard.

"A knife always works," said the Warlock.

"Oh," said Hap.

"I worked the metal myself, with ordinary blacksmith's tools, so the knife wouldn't crumble when the magic was gone. The runes aren't magic. They only say—"

"Oh," said Hap. "Oh." He toppled sideways.

The Warlock lowered himself onto his back. He held the knife up and read the markings, in a language only the Brotherhood remembered.

AND THIS, TOO, SHALL PASS AWAY. It was a very old platitude, even then.

He dropped his arm back and lay looking at the sky.

Presently the blue was blotted by a shadow.

"I told you to get out of here," he whispered.

"You should have known better. What's *happened* to you?"

"No more youth spells. I knew I'd have to do it when the prognostics spell showed blank." He drew a ragged breath. "It was worth it. I killed Glirendree."

"Playing hero, at your age! What can I do? How can I help?"

"Get me down the hill before my heart stops. I never told you my true age—"

"I knew. The whole village knows." She pulled him to sitting position, pulled one of his arms around her neck. It felt dead. She shuddered, but she wrapped her own arm around his waist and gathered herself for the effort. "You're so thin! Come on, love. We're going to stand up." She took most of his weight onto her, and they stood up.

"Go slow. I can hear my heart trying to take off."

"How far do we have to go?"

"Just to the foot of the hill, I think. Then the spells will work again, and we can rest." He stumbled. "I'm going blind," he said.

"It's a smooth path, and all downhill."

"That's why I picked this place. I knew I'd have to use the disc someday. You can't throw away knowledge. Always the time comes when you use it, because you have to, because it's there."

"You've changed so. So—so ugly. And you smell."

107

The pulse fluttered in his neck, like a hummingbird's wings. "Maybe you won't want me, after seeing me like this."

"You can change back, can't you?"

"Sure. I can change to anything you like. What color eyes do you want?"

"I'll be like this myself someday," she said. Her voice held cool horror. And it was fading; he was going deaf.

"I'll teach you the proper spells, when you're ready. They're dangerous. Blackly dangerous."

She was silent for a time. Then: "What color were *his* eyes? You know, Belhap Sattlestone whatever."

"Forget it," said the Warlock, with a touch of pique.

And suddenly his sight was back.

But not forever, thought the Warlock as they stumbled through the sudden daylight. When the mana runs out, I'll go like a blown candle flame, and civilization will follow. No more magic, no more magic-based industries. Then the whole world will be barbarian until men learn a new way to coerce nature, and the swordsmen, the damned stupid swordsmen will win after all.

The story which follows is not one semi so precious as its title might imply; it is, indeed, pretty close to what used to be called "space opera," except stylistically. Its triumph in the voting suggests that the adventure story and the picaresque hero are less out of fashion in science fiction than some recent complainers would have us believe.

TIME CONSIDERED AS A HELIX OF SEMI-PRECIOUS STONES

Samuel R. Delany

Lay ordinate and abscissa on the century. Now cut me a quadrant. Third quadrant if you please. I was born in 'fifty. Here it's 'seventy-five.

At sixteen they let me leave the orphanage. Dragging the name they'd hung me with (Harold Clancy Everet, and me a mere lad—how many monickers have I had since; but don't worry, you'll recognize my smoke) over the hills of East Vermont, I came to a decision:

Me and Pa Michaels, who had belligerently given me a job at the request of *The Official* looking *Document* with which the orphanage sends you packing, were running Pa Michaels' dairy farm, i.e., thirteen thousand three hundred sixty-two piebald Guernseys all asleep in their stainless coffins, nourished and drugged by pink liquid flowing in clear plastic veins (stuff is sticky and messes up your hands), exercised with electric pulsers that make their muscles quiver, them not half awake, and the milk just a-pouring down into stainless cisterns. Anyway. The Deci-

 Nebula Award, Best Novelette 1969

sion (as I stood there in the fields one afternoon like the Man with the Hoe, exhausted with three hard hours of physical labor, contemplating the machinery of the universe through the fog of fatigue): With all of Earth, and Mars, and the Outer Satellites filled up with people and what-all, there had to be something more than this. I decided to get some.

So I stole a couple of Pa's credit cards, one of his helicopters and a bottle of white lightning the geezer made himself, and took off. Ever try to land a stolen helicopter on the roof of the Pan Am building, drunk? Jail, schmail, and some hard knocks later I had attained to wisdom. But remember this oh best beloved: I have done three honest hours on a dairy farm less than ten years back. And nobody has ever called me Harold Clancy Everet again.

Hank Culafroy Eckles (red-headed, a bit vague, six foot two) strolled out of the baggage room at the spaceport carrying a lot of things that weren't his in a small briefcase.

Beside him the Business Man was saying, "You young fellows today upset me. Go back to Bellona, I say. Just because you got into trouble with that little blonde you were telling me about is no reason to leap worlds, come on all glum. Even quit your job!"

Hank stops and grins weakly: "Well . . ."

"Now I admit, you have your real needs, which maybe we older folks don't understand, but you have to show some responsibility toward . . ." He notices Hank has stopped in front of a door marked MEN. "Oh. Well. Eh." He grins strongly. "I've enjoyed meeting you, Hank. It's always nice when you meet somebody worth talking to on these damn crossings. So long."

Out same door, ten minutes later, comes Harmony C. Eventide, six foot even (one of the false heels was cracked, so I stuck both of them under a lot of paper towels), brown hair (not even my hairdresser knows for sure), oh so dapper and of his time, attired in the bad taste that is oh so tasteful, a sort of man with whom no Business Men would start a conversation. Took the regulation 'copter from the port over to the Pan Am building (Yeah. Really. Drunk), came out of Grand Central Station, and strode along Forty-second towards Eighth Avenue, with a lot of things that weren't mine in a small briefcase.

The evening is carved from light.

Crossed the plastiplex pavement of the Great White Way—I think it makes people look weird, all that white light under their chins—and skirted the crowds coming up in elevators from the sub-way, the sub-sub-way, and the sub-sub-sub (eighteen and first week out of jail I hung around here, snatching stuff from people—but daintily, daintily, so they never knew they'd been snatched), bulled my way through a crowd of giggling, goo-chewing school girls with flashing lights in their hair, all very embarrassed at wearing transparent plastic blouses which had just been made legal again (I hear the breast has been scene [as opposed to obscene] on and off since the seventeenth century) so I stared appreciatively; they giggled some more. I thought, Christ, when I was that age, I was on a God damn dairy farm, and took the thought no further.

The ribbon of news lights looping the triangular structure of Communication, Inc., explained in Basic English how Senator Regina Abolafia was preparing to begin her investigation of Organized Crime in the City. Days I'm so happy I'm disorganized I couldn't begin to tell.

Near Ninth Avenue I took my briefcase into a long, crowded bar. I hadn't been in New York for two years, but on my last trip through ofttimes a man used to hang out here who had real talent for getting rid of things that weren't mine profitably, safely, fast. No idea what the chances were I'd find him. I pushed among a lot of guys drinking beer. Here and there were a number of well escorted old bags wearing last month's latest. Scarfs of smoke gentled through the noise. I don't like such places. Those there younger than me were all morphadine heads or feeble minded. Those older only wished more younger ones would come. I pried my way to the bar and tried to get the attention of one of the little men in white coats.

The lack of noise behind me made me glance back—

She wore a sheath of veiling closed at the neck and wrists with huge brass pins (oh so tastefully on the border of taste); her left arm was bare, her right covered with chiffon like wine. She had it down a lot better than I did.

111

But such an ostentatious demonstration of one's under-standing of the fine points was absolutely out of place in a place like this. People were making a great show of not noticing.

She pointed to her wrist, blood-colored nail indexing a yellow-orange fragment in the brass claw of her wrist-let. "Do you know what this is, Mr. Eldrich?" she asked; at the same time the veil across her face cleared, and her eyes were ice; her brows, black.

Three thoughts: (One) She is a lady of fashion, be-cause coming in from Bellona I'd read the *Delta* coverage of the "fading fabrics" whose hue and opacity were con-trolled by cunning jewels at the wrist. (Two) During my last trip through, when I was younger and Harry Cala-mine Eldrich, I didn't do anything *too* illegal (though one loses track of these things); still I didn't believe I could be dragged off to the calaboose for anything more than thirty days under that name. (Three) The stone she pointed to. . . .

". . . Jasper?" I asked.

She waited for me to say more; I waited for her to give me reason to let on I knew what she was waiting for (when I was in jail Henry James was my favorite author. He really was.).

"Jasper," she confirmed.

"—Jasper. . . ." I reopened the ambiguity she had tried so hard to dispel.

". . . Jasper—" But she was already faltering, suspect-ing I suspected her certainty to be ill-founded.

"Okay. Jasper." But from her face I knew she had seen in my face a look that had finally revealed I knew she knew I knew.

"Just whom have you got me confused with, Ma'am?"

Jasper, this month, is the Word.

Jasper is the pass/code/warning that the Singers of the Cities (who, last month, sang "Opal" from their divine injuries; and on Mars I'd heard the Word and used it thrice, along with devious imitations, to fix possession of what was not rightfully my own; and even there I pon-dered Singers and their wounds) relay by word of mouth for that loose and roguish fraternity with which I have been involved (in various guises) these nine years. It goes out new every thirty days; and within hours every brother knows it, throughout six worlds and worldlets. Usually it's grunted at you by some blood-soaked bastard staggering into your arms from a dark doorway; hissed at you as you pass a shadowed alley; scrawled on a paper scrap pressed into your palm by some nasty-grimy moving too fast through the crowd. And this month, it was: Jasper.

Here are some alternate translations:

Help!

or

I need help!

or

I can help you!

or

You are being watched!

or

They're not watching now, so *move!*

Final point of syntax: If the Word is used properly, you should never have to think twice about what it means in a given situation. Fine point of usage: Never trust anyone who uses it improperly.

I waited for her to finish waiting.

She opened a wallet in front of me. "Chief of Special Services Department Maudline Hinkle," she read without looking at what it said below the silver badge.

"You have that very well," I said, "Maud." Then I frowned. "Hinkle?"

"Me."

"I know you're not going to believe this, Maud. You look like a woman who has no patience with her mistakes. But my name is Eventide. Not Eldrich. Harmony C. Eventide. And isn't it lucky for all and sundry that the Word changes tonight?" Passed the way it is, the Word is no big secret to the cops. But I've met policemen up to a week after change date who were not privy.

"Well, then: Harmony. I want to talk to you."

I raised an eyebrow.

She raised one back and said, "Look, if you want to be called Henrietta, it's all right by me. But you listen."

"What do you want to talk about?"

"Crime, Mr. . . . . ?"

"Eventide. I'm going to call you Maud, so you might as well call me Harmony. It really is my name."

Maud smiled. She wasn't a young woman. I think she even had a few years on Business Man. But she used make-up better than he did. "I probably know more about crime than you do," she said. "In fact I wouldn't be surprised if you hadn't even heard of my branch of the police department. What does Special Services mean to you?"

"That's right, I've never heard of it."

"You've been more or less avoiding the Regular Service with alacrity for the past seven years."

"Oh, Maud, really—"

"Special Services is reserved for people whose nuisance value has suddenly taken a sharp rise . . . a sharp enough rise to make our little lights start blinking."

"Surely I haven't done anything so dreadful that—"

"We don't look at what you do. A computer does that for us. We simply keep checking the first derivative of the graphed out curve that bears your number. Your slope is rising sharply."

"Not even the dignity of a name—"

"We're the most efficient department in the Police Organization. Take it as bragging if you wish. Or just a piece of information."

"Well, well, well," I said. "Have a drink?" The little man in the white coat left us two, looked puzzled at Maud's finery, then went to do something else.

"Thanks." She downed half her glass like someone stauncher than that wrist would indicate. "It doesn't pay to go after most criminals. Take your big-time racketeers, Farnesworth, The Hawk, Blavatskia. Take your little snatch-purses, small-time pushers, housebreakers or vice-impresarios. Both at the top and the bottom of the scale, their incomes are pretty stable. They don't really upset the social boat. Regular Services handles them both. They think they do a good job. We're not going to argue. But say a little pusher starts to become a big-time pusher; a medium-sized vice-impresario sets his sights on becoming a full-fledged racketeer; that's when you get problems with socially unpleasant repercussions. That's when Special Services arrive. We have a couple of techniques that work remarkably well."

"You're going to tell me about them, aren't you."

"They work better that way," she said. "One of them is

holgramic information storage. Do you know what happens when you cut a hologram plate in half?"

"The three dimensional image is . . . cut in half?"

She shook her head. "You get the whole image, only fuzzier, slightly out of focus."

"Now I didn't know that."

"And if you cut it in half again, it just gets fuzzier still. But even if you have a square centimeter of the original hologram you still have the whole image—unrecognizable, but complete."

I mumbled some appreciative *m*'s.

"Each pinpoint of photographic emulsion on a hologram plate, unlike a photograph, gives information about the entire scene being hologrammed. By analogy, hologramic information storage simply means that each bit of information we have—about you, let us say—relates to your entire career, your overall situation, the complete set of tensions between you and your environment. Specific facts about specific misdemeanors or felonies we leave to Regular Services. As soon as we have enough of our kind of data, our method is vastly more efficient for keeping track—even predicting—where you are or what you may be up to."

"Fascinating," I said. "One of the most amazing paranoid syndromes I've ever run up against. I mean just starting a conversation with someone in a bar. Often, in a hospital situation, I've encountered stranger—"

"In your past," she said matter of factly, "I see cows and helicopters. In your not too distant future there are helicopters and hawks."

"And tell me, oh Good Witch of the West, just how—" Then I got all upset inside. Because nobody is supposed to know about that stint with Pa Michaels save thee and me. Even the Regular Service who pulled me, out of my mind, from that whirlibird bouncing towards the edge of the Pan Am never got that one from me. I'd eaten the credit cards when I saw them waiting, and the serial numbers had been filed off everything that could have had a serial number on it by someone more competent than I: good Mister Michaels had boasted to me, my first lonely, drunken night at the farm, how he'd gotten the thing in hot from New Hampshire.

115

"But why"—it appalls me the clichés to which anxiety will drive us—"are you telling me all this?"

She smiled and her smile faded behind her veil. "Information is only meaningful when it is shared," said a voice that was hers from the place of her face.

"Hey, look, I—"

"You may be coming into quite a bit of money soon. If I can calculate right, I will have a helicopter full of the city's finest arriving to take you away as you accept it into your hot little hands. That is a piece of information. . . ." She stepped back. Someone stepped between us.

"Hey, Maud—!"

"You can do whatever you want with it."

The bar was crowded enough so that to move quickly was to make enemies. I don't know—I lost her and made enemies. Some weird characters there: with greasy hair that hung in spikes, and three of them had dragons tattooed on their scrawny shoulders, still another with an eye patch, and yet another raked nails black with pitch at my cheek (we're two minutes into a vicious free-for-all, case you missed the transition. I did) and some of the women were screaming. I hit and ducked, and the tenor of the bruhaha changed. Somebody sang, "Jasper!" the way she is supposed to be sung. And it meant the heat (the ordinary, bungling Regular Service I had been eluding these seven years) were on their way. The brawl spilled into the street. I got between two nasty-grimies who were doing things appropriate with one another, but made the edge of the crowd with no more wounds than could be racked up to shaving. The fight had broken into sections. I left one and ran into another that, I realized a moment later, was merely a ring of people standing around somebody who had apparently gotten really messed.

Someone was holding people back.

Somebody else was turning him over.

Curled up in a puddle of blood was the little guy I hadn't seen in two years who used to be so good at getting rid of things not mine.

Trying not to hit people with my briefcase, I ducked between the hub and the bub. When I saw my first ordinary policeman I tried very hard to look like some-

116

body who had just stepped up to see what the rumpus was.

It worked.

I turned down Ninth Avenue, and got three steps into an inconspicuous but rapid lope—

"Hey, wait! Wait up there. . . ."

I recognized the voice (after two years, coming at me just like that, I recognized it) but kept going.

"Wait! It's me, Hawk!"

And I stopped.

You haven't heard his name before in this story; Maud mentioned *the* Hawk, who is a multi-millionaire racketeer basing his operations on a part of Mars I've never been (though he has his claws sunk to the spurs in illegalities throughout the system) and somebody else entirely.

I took three steps back towards the doorway.

A boy's laugh there: "Oh, man. You look like you just did something you shouldn't."

"Hawk?" I asked the shadow.

He was still the age when two years' absence means an inch or so taller.

"You're still hanging out around here?" I asked.

"Sometimes."

He was an amazing kid.

"Look, Hawk, I got to get out of here." I glanced back at the rumpus.

"Get." He stepped down. "Can I come too?"

Funny. "Yeah." It makes me feel very funny him asking that. "Come on."

By the street lamp, half a block down, I saw his hair was still pale as split pine. He could have been a nasty-grimy: very dirty black denim jacket, no shirt beneath; very ripe pair of black-jeans—I mean in the dark you could tell. He went barefoot; and the only way you can tell on a dark street someone's been going barefoot for days in New York is to know already. As we reached the corner, he grinned up at me under the street lamp and shrugged his jacket together over the welts and furrows marring his chest and belly. His eyes were very green. Do you recognize him? If by some failure of information dispersal throughout the worlds and world-

117

lets you haven't, walking beside me beside the Hudson was Hawk the Singer.

"Hey, how long have you been back?"

"A few hours," I told him.

"What'd you bring?"

"Really want to know?"

He shoved his hands into his pockets and cocked his head. "Sure."

I made the sound of an adult exasperated by a child. "All right." We had been walking the waterfront for a block now; there was nobody about. "Sit down." So he straddled the beam along the siding, one foot dangling above the flashing black Hudson. I sat in front of him and ran my thumb around the edge of the briefcase.

Hawk hunched his shoulders and leaned. "Hey . . ." He flashed green questioning at me. "Can I touch?"

I shrugged. "Go ahead."

He grubbed among them with fingers that were all knuckle and bitten nail. He picked two up, put them down, picked up three others. "Hey!" he whispered. "How much are all these worth?"

"About ten times more than I hope to get. I have to get rid of them fast."

He glanced down at his hanging foot. "You could always throw them in the river."

"Don't be dense. I was looking for a guy who used to hang around that bar. He was pretty efficient." And half the Hudson away a water-bound foil skimmed above the foam. On her deck were parked a dozen helicopters —being ferried up to the Patrol Field near Verrazano, no doubt. But for moments I looked back and forth between the boy and the transport, getting all paranoid about Maud. But the boat *mmmmed* into the darkness. "My man got a little cut up this evening."

Hawk put the tips of his fingers in his pockets and shifted his position.

"Which leaves me up tight. I didn't think he'd take them all but at least he could have turned me on to some other people who might."

"I'm going to a party later on this evening"—he paused to gnaw on the wreck of his little fingernail—"where you might be able to sell them. Alexis Spinnel is having a party for Regina Abolafia at Tower Top."

"Tower Top . . . ?" It had been a while since I palled around with Hawk. Hell's Kitchen at ten; Tower Top at midnight—

"I'm just going because Edna Silem will be there."

Edna Silem is New York's eldest Singer.

Senator Abolafia's name had ribboned above me in lights once that evening. And somewhere among the endless magazines I'd perused coming in from Mars I remember Alexis Spinnel's name sharing a paragraph with an awful lot of money.

"I'd like to see Edna again," I said offhandedly. "But she wouldn't remember me." Folk like Spinnel and his social ilk have a little game, I'd discovered during the first leg of my acquaintance with Hawk. He who can get the most Singers of the City under one roof wins. There are five Singers of New York (a tie for second place with Lux on Iapetus). Tokyo leads with seven. "It's a two Singer party?"

"More likely four . . . if I go."

The inaugural ball for the mayor gets four.

I raised the appropriate eyebrow.

"I have to pick up the Word from Edna. It changes tonight."

"All right," I said. "I don't know what you have in mind but I'm game." I closed the case.

We walked back towards Times Square. When we got to Eighth Avenue and the first of the plastiplex, Hawk stopped. "Wait a minute," he said. Then he buttoned his jacket up to his neck. "Okay."

Strolling through the streets of New York with a Singer (two years back I'd spent much time wondering if that were wise for a man of my profession) is probably the best camouflage possible for a man of my profession. Think of the last time you glimpsed your favorite Tri-D star turning the corner of Fifty-seventh. Now be honest. Would you really recognize the little guy in the tweed jacket half a pace behind him?

Half the people we passed in Times Square recognized him. With his youth, funereal garb, black feet and ash pale hair, he was easily the most colorful of Singers. Smiles; narrowed eyes; very few actually pointed or stared.

"Just exactly who is going to be there who might be able to take this stuff off my hands?"

"Well, Alexis prides himself on being something of an adventurer. They might just take his fancy. And he can give you more than you can get peddling them in the street."

"You'll tell him they're all hot?"

"It will probably make the idea that much more intriguing. He's a creep."

"You say so, friend."

We went down into the sub-sub. The man at the change booth started to take Hawk's coin, then looked up. He began three or four words that were unintelligible through his grin, then just gestured us through.

"Oh," Hawk said, "thank you," with ingenuous surprise, as though this were the first, delightful time such a thing had happened. (Two years ago he had told me sagely, "As soon as I start looking like I expect it, it'll stop happening." I was still impressed by the way he wore his notoriety. The time I'd met Edna Silem, and I'd mentioned this, she said with the same ingenuousness, "But that's what we're chosen for.")

In the bright car we sat on the long seat; Hawk's hands were beside him, one foot rested on the other. Down from us a gaggle of bright-bloused goo-chewers giggled and pointed and tried not to be noticed at it. Hawk didn't look at all, and I tried not to be noticed looking.

Dark patterns rushed the window.

Things below the gray floor hummed.

Once a lurch.

Leaning once; we came out of the ground.

Outside, the city tried on its thousand sequins, then threw them away behind the trees of Ft. Tryon. Suddenly the windows across from us grew bright scales. Behind them the girders of a station reeled by. We got out on the platform under a light rain. The sign said TWELVE TOWERS STATION.

By the time we reached the street, however, the shower had stopped. Leaves above the wall shed water down the brick. "If I'd known I was bringing someone I'd have had Alex send a car for us. I told him it was fifty-fifty I'd come."

"Are you sure it's all right for me to tag along, then?"

"Didn't you come up here with me once before?"

"I've even been up here once before that," I said. "Do you still think it's . . ."

He gave me a withering look. Well; Spinnel would be delighted to have Hawk even if he dragged along a whole gang of real nasty-grimies—Singers are famous for that sort of thing. With one more or less presentable thief, Spinnel was getting off light. Beside us rocks broke away into the city. Behind the gate to our left the gardens rolled up towards the first of the towers. The twelve immense, luxury apartment buildings menaced the lower clouds.

"Hawk the Singer," Hawk said into the speaker at the side of the gate. *Clang* and tic-tic-tic and *Clang*. We walked up the path to the doors and doors of glass.

A cluster of men and women in evening dress were coming out. Three tiers of doors away they saw us. You could see them frowning at the guttersnipe who'd somehow gotten into the lobby (for a moment I thought one of them was Maud, because she wore a sheath of the fading fabric, but she turned; beneath her veil her face was dark as roasted coffee); one of the men recognized him, said something to the others. When they passed us they were smiling. Hawk paid about as much attention to them as he had to the girls on the subway. But when they'd passed, he said, "One of those guys was looking at you."

"Yeah. I saw."

"Do you know why?"

"He was trying to figure out whether we'd met before."

"Had you?"

I nodded. "Right about where I met you, only back when I'd just gotten out of jail. I told you I'd been here once before."

"Oh."

Blue carpet covered three-quarters of the lobby. A great pool filled the rest in which a row of twelve foot trellises stood, crowned with flaming braziers. The lobby itself was three stories high, domed and mirror tiled. Twisting smoke curled towards the ornate grill. Broken reflections sagged and recovered on the walls.

The elevator door folded about us its foil petals. There was the distinct feeling of not moving while seventy-five stories shucked down around us.

We got out on the landscaped roof garden. A very tanned, very blond man wearing an apricot jump-suit, from the collar of which emerged a black turtleneck dicky, came down the rocks (artificial) between the ferns (real) growing along the stream (real water; phony current).

"Hello! Hello!" Pause. "I'm terribly glad you decided to come after all." Pause. "For a while I thought you weren't going to make it." The Pauses were to allow Hawk to introduce me. I was dressed so that Spinnel had no way of telling whether I was a miscellaneous Nobel laureate that Hawk happened to have been dining with, or a varlet whose manners and morals were even lower than mine happen to be.

"Shall I take your jacket?" Alexis offered.

Which meant he didn't know Hawk as well as he would like people to think. But I guess he was sensitive enough to realize from the little cold things that happened in the boy's face that he should forget his offer.

He nodded to me, smiling—about all he could do—and we strolled towards the gathering.

Edna Silem was sitting on a transparent inflated hassock. She leaned forward, holding her drink in both hands, arguing politics with the people sitting on the grass before her. She was the first person I recognized (hair of tarnished silver; voice of scrap brass). Jutting from the cuffs of her mannish suit, her wrinkled hands about her goblet, shaking with the intensity of her pronouncements, were heavy with stones and silver. As I ran my eyes back to Hawk, I saw half a dozen whose names/faces sold magazines, music, sent people to the theater (the drama critic for *Delta*, wouldn't you know), and even the mathematician from Princeton I'd read about a few months ago who'd come up with the "quasar/quark" explanation.

There was one woman my eyes kept returning to. On glance three I recognized her as the New Fascistas' most promising candidate for president, Senator Abolafia. Her arms were folded and she was listening intently to the discussion that had narrowed to Edna and an overly

122

gregarious younger man whose eyes were puffy from what could have been the recent acquisition of contact lenses.

"But don't you feel, Mrs. Silem, that—"

"You must remember when you make predictions like that—"

"Mrs. Silem, I've seen statistics that—"

"You *must* remember"—her voice tensed, lowered, till the silence between the words was as rich as the voice was sparse and metallic—"that if everything, *everything* were known, statistical estimates would be unnecessary. The science of probability gives mathematical expression to our ignorance, not to our wisdom," which I was thinking was an interesting second installment to Maud's lecture, when Edna looked up and exclaimed, "Why, Hawk!"

Everyone turned.

"I *am* glad to see you. Lewis, Ann," she called: there were two other Singers there already (he dark, she pale, both tree-slender; their faces made you think of pools without drain or tribute come upon in the forest, clear and very still; husband and wife, they had been made Singers together the day before their marriage seven years ago), "he hasn't deserted us after all!" Edna stood, extended her arm over the heads of the people sitting, and barked across her knuckles as though her voice were a pool cue. "Hawk, there are people here arguing with me who don't know nearly as much as you about the subject. You'd be on my side, now, wouldn't you—"

"Mrs. Silem, I didn't mean to—" from the floor.

Then her arms swung six degrees, her fingers, eyes and mouth opened. "You!" Me. "My dear, if there's anyone I never expected to see here! Why it's been almost two years, hasn't it?" Bless Edna; the place where she and Hawk and I had spent a long, beery evening together had more resembled that bar than Tower Top. "Where have you been keeping yourself?"

"Mars, mostly," I admitted. "Actually I just came back today." It's so much fun to be able to say things like that in a place like this.

"Hawk—both of you—" (which meant either she had forgotten my name, or she remembered me well enough not to abuse it) "come over here and help me drink up Alexis' good liquor." I tried not to grin as we walked

123

towards her. If she remembered anything, she certainly recalled my line of business and must have been enjoying this as much as I was.

Relief spread Alexis' face: he knew now I was *someone* if not *which* someone I was.

As we passed Lewis and Ann, Hawk gave the two Singers one of his luminous grins. They returned shadowed smiles. Lewis nodded. Ann made a move to touch his arm, but left the motion unconcluded; and the company noted the interchange.

Having found out what we wanted, Alex was preparing large glasses of it over crushed ice when the puffy-eyed gentleman stepped up for a refill. "But, Mrs. Silem, then what do you feel validly opposes such political abuses?"

Regina Abolafia wore a white silk suit. Nails, lips and hair were one color; and on her breast was a worked copper pin. It's always fascinated me to watch people used to being the center thrust to the side. She swirled her glass, listening.

"I oppose them," Edna said. "Hawk opposes them. Lewis and Ann oppose them. We, ultimately, are what you have." And her voice had taken on that authoritative resonance only Singers can assume.

Then Hawk's laugh snarled through the conversational fabric.

We turned.

He'd sat cross-legged near the hedge. "Look . . ." he whispered.

Now people's gazes followed his. He was looking at Lewis and Ann. She, tall and blonde, he, dark and taller, were standing very quietly, a little nervously, eyes closed (Lewis' lips were apart).

"Oh," whispered someone who should have known better, "they're going to . . ."

I watched Hawk because I'd never had a chance to observe one Singer at another's performance. He put the soles of his feet together, grasped his toes and leaned forward, veins making blue rivers on his neck. The top button of his jacket had come loose. Two scar ends showed over his collarbone. Maybe nobody noticed but me.

I saw Edna put her glass down with a look of beaming anticipatory pride. Alex, who had pressed the autobar (odd how automation has become the upper crust's way of flaunting the labor surplus) for more crushed ice, looked up, saw what was about to happen, and pushed the cut-off button. The autobar hummed to silence. A breeze (artificial or real, I couldn't tell you) came by and the trees gave us a final *shush*.

One at a time, then in duet, then singly again, Lewis and Ann sang.

Singers are people who look at things, then go and tell people what they've seen. What makes them Singers is their ability to make people listen. That is the most magnificent over-simplification I can give. Eighty-six-year-old El Posado, in Rio de Janeiro, saw a block of tenements collapse, ran to the Avenida del Sol and began improvising, in rhyme and meter (not all that hard in rhyme-rich Portuguese), tears runneling his dusty cheeks, his voice clashing with the palm swards above the sunny street. Hundreds of people stopped to listen; a hundred more; and another hundred. And they told hundreds more what they had heard. Three hours later, hundreds from among them had arrived at the scene with blankets, food, money, shovels and, more incredibly, the willingness and ability to organize themselves and work within that organization. No Tri-D report of a disaster has ever produced that sort of reaction. El Posado is historically considered the first Singer. The second was Miriamne in the roofed city of Lux, who for thirty years walked through the metal streets singing the glories of the rings of Saturn—the colonists can't look at them without aid because of the ultraviolet the rings set up. But Miriamne, with her strange cataracts, each dawn, walked to the edge of the city, looked, saw and came back to sing of what she saw. All of which would have meant nothing except that during the days she did not sing—through illness, or once she was on a visit to another city to which her fame had spread—the Lux Stock Exchange would go down, the number of violent crimes rise. Nobody could explain it. All they could do was proclaim her Singer. Why did the institution of Singers come about, springing up in just about every urban center throughout the system? Some have speculated that it was a spontaneous reaction to the mass media which blanket our lives. While Tri-D and radio and news-tapes disperse information all over the worlds, they also spread a sense of alienation from first-hand experience. (How many people still go to sports events or a political rally with their little receivers plugged to their ears to let them know that what they see is really happening?) The first Singers were proclaimed by the people around them. Then, there was a period where anyone could proclaim himself who wanted to, and people either responded to him, or laughed him into oblivion. But by the time I was left on the doorstep of somebody who didn't want me, most cities had more or less established an unofficial quota. When a position is left open today, the remaining Singers choose who is going to fill it. The required talents are poetic, theatrical, as well as a certain charisma that is generated in the tensions between the personality and the publicity web a Singer is immediately snared in. Before he became a Singer, Hawk had gained something of a prodigious reputation with a book of poems published when he was fifteen. He was touring universities and giving readings, but the reputation was still small enough so that he was amazed that I had ever heard of him, that evening we encountered in Central Park (I had just spent a pleasant thirty days as a guest of the city and it's amazing what you find in the Tombs Library). It was a few weeks after his sixteenth birthday. His Singership was to be announced in four days, though he had been informed already. We sat by the lake till dawn, while he weighed and pondered and agonized over the coming responsibility. Two years later, he's still the youngest Singer in six worlds by half a dozen years. Before becoming a Singer, a person need not have been a poet, but most are either that or actors, But the roster through the system includes a longshoreman, two university professors, an heiress to the Silitax millions (Tack it down with Sili-tacks), and at least two persons of such dubious background that the ever-hungry-for-sensation Publicity Machine itself has agreed not to let any of it past the copy-editors. But wherever their origins, these diverse and flamboyant living myths sang of love, of death, the changing of seasons, social classes, governments and the palace guard. They sang before large crowds, small ones, to an individual laborer coming home from the city's docks, on slum street corners, in club cars of commuter trains, in the elegant gardens atop Twelve Towers, to Alex Spinnel's select soirée. But it has been illegal to reproduce the "Songs" of the Singers by mechanical means (including publishing the lyrics) since the institution arose, and I respect the law, I do, as only a man in my profession can. I offer the explanation then in place of Lewis' and Ann's song.

They finished, opened their eyes, stared about with expressions that could have been embarrassment, could have been contempt.

Hawk was leaning forward with a look of rapt approval. Edna was smiling politely. I had the sort of grin on my face that breaks out when you've been vastly moved and vastly pleased. Lewis and Ann had sung superbly.

Alex began to breathe again, glanced around to see what state everybody else was in, saw, and pressed the autobar, which began to hum and crush ice. No clapping, but the appreciative sounds began; people were nodding, commenting, whispering. Regina Abolafia went over to Lewis to say something. I tried to listen until Alex shoved a glass into my elbow.

"Oh, I'm sorry . . ."

I transferred my briefcase to the other hand and took the drink smiling. When Senator Abolafia left the two Singers, they were holding hands and looking at one another a little sheepishly. They sat down again.

The party drifted in conversational groups through the gardens, through the groves. Overhead clouds the color of old chamois folded and unfolded across the moon.

For a while I stood alone in a circle of trees listening to the misic: a de Lassus two-part canon, programmed for audio-generators. Recalled: an article in one of last week's large-circulation literaries stating that it was the only way to remove the feel of the bar lines imposed by five centuries of meter on modern musicians. For another two weeks this would be acceptable entertainment. The trees circled a rock pool; but no water. Below the plastic surface, abstract lights wove and threaded in a shifting lumia.

"Excuse me . . . ?"

I turned to see Alexis, who had no drink now or idea what to do with his hands. He *was* nervous.

". . . but our young friend has told me you have something I might be interested in."

I started to lift my briefcase, but Alex's hand came down from his ear (it had gone by belt to hair to collar already) to halt me. Nouveau riche.

"That's all right. I don't need to see them yet. In fact, I'd rather not. I have something to propose to you. I would certainly be interested in what you have if they are, indeed, as Hawk has described them. But I have a guest here who would be even more curious."

That sounded odd.

"I know that sounds odd," Alexis assessed, "but I thought you might be interested simply because of the finances involved. I am an eccentric collector who would offer you a price concomitant with what I would use them for: eccentric conversation pieces—and because of the nature of the purchase I would have to limit severely the people with whom I could converse."

I nodded.

"My guest, however, would have a great deal more use for them."

"Could you tell me who this guest is?"

"I asked Hawk, finally, who you were and he led me to believe I was on the verge of a grave social indiscretion. It would be equally indiscreet to reveal my guest's name to you." He smiled. "But indiscretion is the better part of the fuel that keeps the social machine turning, Mr. Harvey Cadwaliter-Erickson. . . ." He smiled knowingly.

I have *never* been Harvey Cadwaliter-Erickson, but then, Hawk was always an inventive child. Then a second thought went by, vid., the tungsten magnates, the Cadwaliter-Ericksons of Tythis on Triton. Hawk was not only inventive, he was as brilliant as all the magazines and newspapers are always saying he is.

"I assume your second indiscretion will be to tell me who this mysterious guest is?"

"Well," Alex said with the smile of the canary-fattened cat, "Hawk agreed with me that *the* Hawk might well be curious as to what you have in there," (he pointed) "as indeed he is."

I frowned. Then I thought lots of small, rapid thoughts I'll articulate in due time. *"The* Hawk?"

Alex nodded.

I don't think I was actually scowling. "Would you send our young friend up here for a moment?"

"If you'd like." Alex bowed, turned. Perhaps a minute later, Hawk came up over the rocks and through the trees, grinning. When I didn't grin back, he stopped.

"Mmmm . . ." I began.

His head cocked.

I scratched my chin with a knuckle. ". . . Hawk," I said, "are you aware of a department of the police called Special Services?"

"I've heard of them."

"They've suddenly gotten very interested in me."

"Gee," he said with honest amazement. "They're supposed to be effective."

"Mmmm," I reiterated.

"Say," Hawk announced, "how do you like that? My namesake is here tonight. Wouldn't you know."

"Alex doesn't miss a trick. Have you any idea *why* he's here?"

"Probably trying to make some deal with Abolafia. Her investigation starts tomorrow."

"Oh." I thought over some of those things I had thought before. "Do you know a Maud Hinkle?"

His puzzled look said "no" pretty convincingly.

"She bills herself as one of the upper echelon in the arcane organization of which I spoke."

"Yeah?"

"She ended our interview earlier this evening with a little homily about hawks and helicopters. I took our subsequent encounter as a fillip of coincidence. But now I discover that the evening has confirmed her intimations of plurality." I shook my head. "Hawk, I am suddenly catapulted into a paranoid world where the walls not only have ears, but probably eyes, and long, claw-tipped fingers. Anyone about me—yea, even very you—could turn out to be a spy. I suspect every sewer grating and second-story window conceals binoculars, a tommygun, or worse. What I just can't figure out is how these insidious forces, ubiquitous and omnipresent though they be, induced you to lure me into this intricate and diabolical—"

"Oh, cut it out!" He shook back his hair. "I didn't lure—"

"Perhaps not consciously, but Special Services has Hologramic Information Storage, and their methods are insidious and cruel—"

"I said cut it out." And all sorts of hard little things happened again. "Do you think I'd—" Then he realized how scared I was, I guess. "Look, the Hawk isn't some small time snatch-purse. He lives in just as paranoid a world as you're in now, only all the time. If he's here you can be sure there are just as many of his men—eyes and ears and fingers—as there are of Maud Hickenlooper."

"Hinkle."

"Anyway, it works both ways. No Singer's going to— Look, do you really think I would—"

And even though I knew all those hard little things were scabs over pain, I said, "Yes."

"You did something for me once, and I—"

"I gave you some more welts. That's all."

All the scabs pulled off.

"Hawk," I said. "Let me see."

He took a breath. Then he began to open the brass buttons. The flaps of his jacket fell back. The lumia colored his chest with pastel shiftings.

I felt my face wrinkle. I didn't want to look away. I drew a hissing breath instead, which was just as bad.

He looked up. "There're a lot more than when you were here last aren't there?"

"You're going to kill yourself, Hawk."

He shrugged.

"I can't even tell which are the ones I put there anymore."

He started to point them out.

"Oh, come on," I said, too sharply. And for the length of three breaths, he grew more and more uncomfortable, till I saw him start to reach for the bottom button. "Boy," I said, trying to keep despair out of my voice, "why do you do it?" and ended up keeping out everything. There is nothing more despairing than a voice empty.

He shrugged, saw I didn't want that, and for a moment anger flickered in his green eyes. I didn't want that either. So he said: "Look . . . you touch a person, softly, gently, and maybe you even do it with love. And, well, I guess a

130

piece of information goes on up to the brain where something interprets it as pleasure. Maybe something up there in my head interprets the information all wrong. . . ."

I shook my head. "You're a Singer. Singers are supposed to be eccentric, sure; but—"

Now he was shaking his head. Then the anger opened up. And I saw an expression move from all those spots that had communicated pain through the rest of his features, and vanish without ever becoming a word. Once more he looked down at the wounds that webbed his thin body.

"Button it up, boy. I'm sorry I said anything."

Halfway up the lapels his hands stopped. "You really think I'd turn you in?"

"Button it up."

He did. Then he said, "Oh." And then, "You know, it's midnight."

"Edna just gave me the Word."

"Which is?"

"Agate."

I nodded.

He finished closing his collar. "What are you thinking about?"

"Cows."

"Cows?" Hawk asked. "What about them?"

"You ever been on a dairy farm?"

He shook his head.

"To get the most milk, you keep the cows practically in suspended animation. They're fed intravenously from a big tank that pipes nutrients out and down, branching into smaller and smaller pipes until it gets to all those high yield semi-corpses."

"I've seen pictures."

"People."

". . . and cows?"

"You've given me the Word. And now it begins to funnel down, branching out, with me telling others, and them telling still others, till by midnight tomorrow . . ."

"I'll go get the—"

"Hawk?"

He turned back. "What?"

"You say you don't think I'm going to be the victim of any hanky-panky with the mysterious forces that know

131

more than we— Okay, that's your opinion. But as soon as I get rid of this stuff, I'm going to make the most distracting exit you've ever seen."

Two little lines bit down Hawk's forehead. "Are you sure I haven't seen this one before?"

"As a matter of fact I think you have." Now I grinned.

"Oh," Hawk said, then made a sound that had the structure of laughter but was all breath. "I'll get the Hawk."

He ducked out between the trees.

I glanced up at the lozenges of moonlight in the leaves. I looked down at my briefcase.

Up between the rocks, stepping around the long grass, came the Hawk. He wore a gray evening suit; a gray silk turtleneck. Above his craggy face his head was completely shaved.

"Mr. Cadwaliter-Erickson?" He held out his hand.

I shook: small sharp bones in loose skin. "Does one call you Mr. . . . ?"

"Arty."

"Arty the Hawk." I tried to look like I wasn't giving his gray attire the once-over.

He smiled. "Arty the Hawk. Yeah. I picked that name up when I was younger than our friend down there. Alex says you got . . . well, some things that are not exactly yours. That don't belong to you."

I nodded.

"Show them to me."

"You were told what—"

He brushed away the end of my sentence. "Come on, let me see."

He extended his hand, smiling affably as a bank clerk. I ran my thumb around the pressure-zip. The cover went *tsk*. "Tell me," I said, looking up at his head still lowered to see what I had, "what does one do about Special Services? They seem to be after me."

The head came up. Surprise changed slowly to a craggy leer. "Why, Mr. Cadwaliter-Erickson!" He gave me the up and down openly. "Keep your income steady. Keep it steady, that's one thing you can do."

"If you buy these for anything like what they're worth, that's going to be a little difficult."

"I would imagine. I could always give you less money—"

The cover went *tsk* again.

"—or, barring that, you could try to use your head and outwit them."

"You must have outwitted them at one time or another. You may be on an even keel now, but you had to get there from somewhere else."

Arty the Hawk's nod was downright sly. "I guess you've had a run-in with Maud. Well, I suppose congratulations are in order. And condolences. I always like to do what's in order."

"You seem to know how to take care of yourself. I mean I notice you're not out there mingling with the guests."

"There are two parties going on here tonight," Arty said. "Where do you think Alex disappears off to every five minutes?"

I frowned.

"That lumia down in the rocks"—he pointed towards my feet—"is a mandala of shifting hues on our ceiling. Alex," he chuckled, "goes scuttling off under the rocks where there is a pavilion of Oriental splendor—"

"—and a separate guest list at the door?"

"Regina is on both. I'm on both. So's the kid, Edna, Lewis, Ann—"

"Am I supposed to know all this?"

"Well, you came with a person on both lists. I just thought. . . ." He paused.

I was coming on wrong. Well. A quick change artist learns fairly quick that the verisimilitude factor in imitating someone up the scale is your confidence in your unalienable right to come on wrong. "I'll tell you," I said. "How about exchanging these"—I held out the briefcase —"for some information."

"You want to know how to stay out of Maud's clutches?" In a moment he shook his head. "It would be pretty stupid of me to tell you, even if I could. Besides, you've got your family fortunes to fall back on." He beat the front of his shirt with his thumb. "Believe me, boy. Arty the Hawk didn't have that. I didn't have anything like that." His hands dropped into his pockets. "Let's see what you got."

I opened the case again.

The Hawk looked for a while. After a few moments he

133

picked a couple up, turned them around, put them back down, put his hands back in his pockets. "I'll give you sixty thousand for them, approved credit tablets."

"What about the information I wanted?"

"I wouldn't tell you a thing." He smiled. "I wouldn't tell you the time of day."

There are very few successful thieves in this world. Still less on the other five. The will to steal is an impulse towards the absurd and the tasteless. (The talents are poetic, theatrical, a certain reverse charisma. . . .) But it is a will, as the will to order, power, love.

"All right," I said.

Somewhere overhead I heard a faint humming.

Arty looked at me fondly. He reached under the lapel of his jacket, and took out a handful of credit tablets— the scarlet-banded tablets whose slips were ten thousand apiece. He pulled off one. Two. Three. Four.

"You can deposit this much safely—?"

"Why do you think Maud is after me?"

Five. six.

"Fine," I said.

"How about throwing in the briefcase?" Arty asked.

"Ask Alex for a paper bag. If you want, I can send them—"

"Give them here."

The humming was coming closer.

I held up the open case. Arty went in with both hands. He shoved them into his coat pockets, his pants pockets; the gray cloth was distended by angular bulges. He looked left, right. "Thanks," he said. "Thanks." Then he turned, and hurried down the slope with all sorts of things in his pockets that weren't his now.

I looked up through the leaves for the noise, but I couldn't see anything.

I stooped down now and laid my case open. I pulled open the back compartment where I kept the things that did belong to me, and rummaged hurriedly through.

Alex was just offering Puffy-eyes another scotch, while the gentleman was saying, "Has anyone seen Mrs. Silem? What's that humming overhead—?" when a large woman wrapped in a veil of fading fabric tottered across the rocks, screaming.

Her hands were clawing at her covered face.

Alex sloshed soda over his sleeve and the man said, "Oh my God! Who's that?"

"No!" the woman shrieked. "Oh no! Help me!" waving her wrinkled fingers, brilliant with rings.

"Don't you recognize her?" That was Hawk whispering confidentially to someone else. "It's Henrietta, Countess of Effingham."

And Alex, overhearing, went hurrying to her assistance. The Countess, however, ducked between two cacti, and disappeared into the high grass. But the entire party followed. They were beating about the underbrush when a balding gentleman in a black tux, bow tie, and cummerbund coughed and said, in a very worried voice, "Excuse me, Mr. Spinnel?"

Alex whirled.

"Mr. Spinnel, my mother . . ."

"Who are *you?*" The interruption upset Alex terribly. The gentleman drew himself up to announce: "The Honorable Clement Effingham," and his pants legs shook for all the world as if he had started to click his heels. But articulation failed. The expression melted on his face. "Oh, I . . . my mother, Mr. Spinnel. We were downstairs, at the other half of your party, when she got very upset. She ran up here—oh, I told her not to! I knew you'd be upset. But you must help me!" and then looked up.

The others looked too.

The helicopter blacked the moon, doffing and settling below its hazy twin parasols.

"Oh, please . . ." the gentleman said. "You look over there! Perhaps she's gone back down. I've got to"—looking quickly both ways—"find her." He hurried in one direction while everyone else hurried in others.

The humming was suddenly syncopated with a crash. Roaring now, as plastic fragments from the transparent roof chattered down through the branches, clattered on the rocks . . .

I made it into the elevator and had already thumbed the edge of my briefcase clasp, when Hawk dove between the unfolding foils. The electric-eye began to swing them open. I hit DOOR CLOSE full fist.

The boy staggered, banged shoulders on two walls, then got back breath and balance. "Hey, there's police getting out of that helicopter!"

"Hand-picked by Maud Hinkle herself, no doubt." I pulled the other tuft of white hair from my temple. It went into the case on top of the plastiderm gloves (wrinkled, thick blue veins, long carnelian nails) that had been Henrietta's hands, lying in the chiffon folds of her sari.

Then there was the downward tug of stopping. The Honorable Clement was still half on my face when the door opened.

Gray and gray, with an absolutely dismal expression on his face, the Hawk swung through the doors. Behind him people were dancing in an elaborate pavilion festooned with Oriental magnificence (and a mandala of shifting hues on the ceiling.) Arty beat me to DOOR CLOSE. Then he gave me an odd look.

I just sighed and finished peeling off Clem.

"The police are up there?" the Hawk reiterated.

"Arty," I said, buckling my pants, "it certainly looks that way." The car gained momentum. "You look almost as upset as Alex." I shrugged the tux jacket down my arms, turning the sleeves inside out, pulled one wrist free, and jerked off the white starched dicky with the black bow tie and stuffed it into the briefcase with all my other dickies; swung the coat around and slipped on Howard Calvin Evingston's good gray herringbone. Howard (like Hawk) is a redhead (but not as curly).

The Hawk raised his bare brows when I peeled off Clement's bald pate and shook out my hair.

"I noticed you aren't carrying around all those bulky things in your pocket any more."

"Oh, those have been taken care of," he said gruffly. "They're all right."

"Arty," I said, adjusting my voice down to Howard's security-provoking, ingenuous baritone, "it must have been my unabashed conceit that made me think that those Regular Service police were here just for me—"

The Hawk actually snarled. "They wouldn't be that unhappy if they got me, too."

And from his corner Hawk demanded, "You've got security here with you, don't you, Arty?"

"So what?"

"There's one way you can get out of this," Hawk hissed at me. His jacket had come half open down his wrecked chest. "That's if Arty takes you out with him."

"Brilliant idea," I concluded. "You want a couple of thousand back for the service?"

The idea didn't amuse him. "I don't want anything from you." He turned to Hawk. "I need something from you, kid. Not him. Look, I wasn't prepared for Maud. If you want me to get your friend out, then you've got to do something for me."

The boy looked confused.

I thought I saw smugness on Arty's face, but the expression resolved into concern. "You've got to figure out some way to fill the lobby up with people, and fast."

I was going to ask why but then I didn't know the extent of Arty's security. I was going to ask how but the floor pushed up at my feet and the doors swung open. "If you can't do it," the Hawk growled to Hawk, "none of us will get out of here. None of us!"

I had no idea what the kid was going to do, but when I started to follow him out into the lobby, the Hawk grabbed my arm and hissed, "Stay here, you idiot!!"

I stepped back. Arty was leaning on DOOR OPEN.

Hawk sprinted towards the pool. And splashed in.

He reached the braziers on their twelve foot tripods and began to climb.

"He's going to hurt himself!" the Hawk whispered.

"Yeah," I said, but I don't think my cynicism got through. Below the great dish of fire, Hawk was fiddling. Then something under there came loose. Something else went *Clang!* And something else spurted out across the water. The fire raced along it and hit the pool, churning and roaring like hell.

A black arrow with a golden head: Hawk dove.

I bit the inside of my cheek as the alarm sounded. Four people in uniforms were coming across the blue carpet. Another group were crossing in the other direction, saw the flames, and one of the women screamed. I let out my breath, thinking carpet and walls and ceiling would be flame-proof. But I kept losing focus on the idea before the sixty-odd infernal feet.

Hawk surfaced on the edge of the pool in the only

clear spot left, rolled over on to the carpet, clutching his face. And rolled. And rolled. Then, came to his feet.

Another elevator spilled out a load of passengers who gaped and gasped. A crew came through the doors now with fire-fighting equipment. The alarm was still sounding.

Hawk turned to look at the dozen-odd people in the lobby. Water puddled the carpet about his drenched and shiny pants legs. Flame turned the drops on his cheek and hair to flickering copper and blood.

He banged his fists against his wet thighs, took a deep breath, and against the roar and the bells and the whispering, he Sang.

Two people ducked back into two elevators. From a doorway half a dozen more emerged. The elevators returned half a minute later with a dozen people each. I realized the message was going through the building, there's a Singer Singing in the lobby.

The lobby filled. The flames growled, the fire fighters stood around shuffling, and Hawk, feet apart on the blue rug, by the burning pool Sang, and Sang of a bar off Times Square full of thieves, morphadine-heads, brawlers, drunkards, women too old to trade what they still held out for barter, and trade just too nasty-grimy, where, earlier in the evening, a brawl had broken out, and an old man had been critically hurt in the fray.

Arty tugged at my sleeve.

"What . . . ?"

"Come on," he hissed.

The elevator door closed behind us.

We ambled through the attentive listeners, stopping to watch, stopping to hear. I couldn't really do Hawk justice. A lot of that slow amble I spent wondering what sort of security Arty had:

Standing behind a couple in a bathrobe who were squinting into the heat, I decided it was all very simple. Arty wanted simply to drift away through a crowd, so he'd conveniently gotten Hawk to manufacture one.

To get to the door we had to pass through practically a cordon of Regular Service policemen who I don't think had anything to do with what might have been going on in the roof garden; they'd simply collected to see the fire and stayed for the Song. When Arty tapped one on the shoulder, "Excuse me please," to get by, the policeman glanced at him, glanced away, then did a Mack Sennet double-take. But another policeman caught the whole interchange, and touched the first on the arm and gave him a frantic little headshake. Then both men turned very deliberately back to watch the Singer. While the earthquake in my chest stilled, I decided that the Hawk's security complex of agents and counter agents, maneuvering and machinating through the flaming lobby, must be of such finesse and intricacy that to attempt understanding was to condemn oneself to total paranoia.

Arty opened the final door.

I stepped from the last of the air conditioning into the night.

We hurried down the ramp.

"Hey, Arty . . . ?"

"You go that way." He pointed down the street. "I go this way."

"Eh . . . what's that way?" I pointed in my direction.

"Twelve Towers sub-sub-subway station. Look. I've got you out of there. Believe me, you're safe for the time being. Now go take a train someplace interesting. Goodbye. Go on now." Then Arty the Hawk put his fists in his pockets and hurried up the street.

I started down, keeping near the wall, expecting someone to get me with a blow-dart from a passing car, a deathray from the shrubbery.

I reached the sub.

And still nothing had happened.

Agate gave way to Malachite:

Tourmaline:

Beryl (during which month I turned twenty-six):

Porphyry:

Sapphire (that month I took the ten thousand I hadn't frittered away and invested it in The Glacier, a perfectly legitimate ice cream palace on Triton—the first and only ice cream palace on Triton—which took off like fireworks; all investors were returned eight hundred percent, no kidding. Two weeks later I'd lost half of those earnings on another set of preposterous illegalities, and was feeling quite depressed, but The Glacier kept pulling them in. The new Word came by):

Cinnabar:

Turquoise:

Tiger's Eye:

Hector Calhoun Eisenhower finally buckled down and spent these three months learning how to be a respectable member of the upper middle class underworld. That is a long novel in itself. High finance; corporate law; how to hire help: Whew! But the complexities of life have always intrigued me. I got through it. The basic rule is still the same: observe carefully, imitate effectively.

Garnet:

Topaz (I whispered that word on the roof of the Trans-Satellite Power Station, and caused my hirelings to commit two murders. And you know? I didn't feel a thing):

Taafite:

We were nearing the end of Taafite. I'd come back to Triton on strictly Glacial business. A bright pleasant morning it was: the business went fine. I decided to take off the afternoon and go sight-seeing in the Torrents.

". . . two hundred and thirty yards high," the guide announced and everyone around me leaned on the rail and gazed up through the plastic corridor at the cliffs of frozen methane that soared through Neptune's cold green glare.

"Just a few yards down the catwalk, ladies and gentlemen, you can catch your first glimpse of the Well of This World, where, over a million years ago, a mysterious force science still cannot explain caused twenty-five square miles of frozen methane to liquefy for no more than a few hours during which time a whirlpool twice the depth of Earth's Grand Canyon was caught for the ages when the temperature dropped once more to . . ."

People were moving down the corridor when I saw her smiling. My hair was black and nappy and my skin was chestnut dark today.

I was just feeling overconfident, I guess, so I kept standing around next to her. I even contemplated coming on. Then she broke the whole thing up by suddenly turning to me and saying, perfectly deadpan: "Why, if it isn't Hamlet Caliban Enobarbus!"

Old reflexes realigned my features to couple the frown of confusion with the smile of indulgence. *Pardon me, but I think you must have mistaken . . .* No, I didn't say it.

"Maud," I said, "have you come here to tell me that my time has come?"

She wore several shades of blue, with a large blue brooch at her shoulder, obviously glass. Still, I realized as I looked about the other tourists, she was more inconspicuous amidst their finery than I was. "No," she said. "Actually I'm on vacation. Just like you."

"No kidding?" We had dropped behind the crowd. "You are kidding."

"Special Services of Earth, while we cooperate with Special Services on other worlds, has no official jurisdiction on Triton. And since you came here with money, and most of your recorded gain in income has been through The Glacier, while Regular Services on Triton might be glad to get you, Special Services is not after you as yet." She smiled. "I haven't been to The Glacier. It would really be nice to say I'd been taken there by one of the owners. Could we go for a soda, do you think?"

The swirled sides of the Well of This World dropped away in opalescent grandeur. Tourists gazed and the guide went on about indices of refraction, angles of incline.

"I don't think you trust me," Maud said.

My look said she was right.

"Have you ever been involved with narcotics?" she asked suddenly.

I frowned.

"No, I'm serious. I want to try and explain something . . . a point of information that may make both our lives easier."

"Peripherally," I said. "I'm sure you've got down all the information in your dossiers."

"I was involved with them a good deal more than peripherally for several years," Maud said. "Before I got into Special Services, I was in the Narcotics Division of the regular force. And the people we dealt with twenty-four hours a day were drug users, drug pushers. To catch the big ones we had to make friends with the little ones. To catch the bigger ones, we had to make friends with the big. We had to keep the same hours they kept, talk the same language, for months at a time live on the same streets, in the same building." She stepped back from the rail to let a youngster ahead. "I had to be sent away to take the morphadine de-toxification cure twice while I

141

was on the narco squad. And I had a better record than most."

"What's your point?"

"Just this. You and I are traveling in the same circles now, if only because of our respective chosen professions. You'd be surprised how many people we already know in common. Don't be shocked when we run into each other crossing Sovereign Plaza in Bellona one day, then two weeks later wind up at the same restaurant for lunch at Lux on Iapetus. Though the circles we move in cover worlds, they *are* the same, and not that big."

"Come on." I don't think I sounded happy. "Let me treat you to that ice cream." We started back down the walkway.

"You know," Maud said, "if you do stay out of Special Services' hands here and on Earth long enough, eventually you'll be up there with a huge income growing on a steady slope. It might be a few years, but it's possible. There's no reason now for us to be *personal* enemies. You just may, someday, reach that point where Special Services loses interest in you as quarry. Oh, we'd still see each other, run into each other. We get a great deal of our information from people up there. We're in a position to help you too, you see."

"You've been casting holograms again."

She shrugged. Her face looked positively ghostly under the pale planet. She said, when we reached the artificial lights of the city, "I did meet two friends of yours recently, Lewis and Ann."

"The Singers?"

She nodded.

"Oh, I don't really know them well."

"They seem to know a lot about you. Perhaps through that other Singer, Hawk."

"Oh," I said again. "Did they say how he was?"

"I read that he was recovering about two months back. But nothing since then."

"That's about all I know too," I said.

"The only time I've ever seen him," Maud said, "was right after I pulled him out."

Arty and I had gotten out of the lobby before Hawk actually finished. The next day on the news-tapes I learned

142

that when his Song was over, he shrugged out of his jacket, dropped his pants, and walked back into the pool.

The fire-fighter crew suddenly woke up; people began running around and screaming: he'd been rescued, seventy percent of his body covered with second and third degree burns. I'd been industriously not thinking about it.

"*You* pulled him out?"

"Yes. I was in the helicopter that landed on the roof," Maud said. "I thought you'd be impressed to see me."

"Oh," I said. "How did you get to pull him out?"

"Once you got going, Arty's security managed to jam the elevator service above the seventy-first floor, so we didn't get to the lobby till after you were out of the building. That's when Hawk tried to—"

"But it was you actually saved him, though?"

"The firemen in that neighborhood hadn't had a fire in twelve years! I don't think they even knew how to operate the equipment. I had my boys foam the pool, then I waded in and dragged him—"

"Oh," I said again. I had been trying hard, almost succeeding, these eleven months. I wasn't there when it happened. It wasn't my affair. Maud was saying:

"We thought we might have gotten a lead on you from him. but when I got him to the shore, he was completely out, just a mass of open, running—"

"I should have known the Special Services uses Singers too," I said. "Everyone else does. The Word changes today, doesn't it? Lewis and Ann didn't pass on what the new one is?"

"I saw them yesterday, and the Word doesn't change for another eight hours. Besides, they wouldn't tell me, anyway." She glanced at me and frowned. "They really wouldn't."

"Let's go have some sodas," I said. "We'll make small talk, and listen carefully to each other, while we affect an air of nonchalance; you will try to pick up things that will make it easier to catch me; I will listen for things you let slip that might make it easier for me to avoid you."

"Um-hm." She nodded.

"Why did you contact me in that bar, anyway?"

Eyes of ice: "I told you, we simply travel in the same

143

circles. We're quite likely to be in the same bar on the same night."

"I guess that's just one of the things I'm not supposed to understand, huh?"

Her smile was appropriately ambiguous. I didn't push it.

It was a very dull afternoon. I couldn't repeat one exchange from the nonsense we babbled over the cherry peaked mountains of whipped cream. We both exerted so much energy to keep up the appearance of being amused, I doubt either one of us could see our way to picking up anything meaningful; if anything meaningful was said.

She left. I brooded some more on the charred phoenix.

The Steward of The Glacier called me into the kitchen to ask about a shipment of contraband milk (The Glacier makes all its own ice cream) that I had been able to wangle on my last trip to Earth (it's amazing how little progress there has been in dairy farming over the last ten years; it was depressingly easy to hornswoggle that bumbling Vermonter) and under the white lights and great plastic churning vats, while I tried to get things straightened out, he made some comment about the Heist Cream Emperor; that didn't do *any* good.

By the time the evening crowd got there, and the moog was making music and the crystal walls were blazing; and the floor show—a new addition that week—had been cajoled into going on anyway (a trunk of costumes had gotten lost in shipment [or swiped, but I wasn't about to tell them that]), and wandering through the tables I, personally, had caught a very grimy little girl, obviously out of her head on morph, trying to pick up a customer's pocketbook from the back of a chair—I just caught her by the wrist, made her let go, and led her to the door, daintily, while she blinked at me with dilated eyes and the customer never even knew—and the floor show, having decided what the hell, were doing their act *au naturel,* and everyone was having just a high old time, I was feeling really bad.

I went outside, sat on the wide steps, and growled when I had to move aside to let people in or out. About the seventy-fifth growl, the person I growled at stopped

144

and boomed down at me, "I thought I'd find you if I looked hard enough! I mean if I really looked."

I looked at the hand that was flapping at my shoulder, followed the arm up to a black turtleneck, where there was a beefy, bald, grinning head. "Arty," I said, "what are . . . ?" But he was still flapping and laughing with impervious *Gemütlichkeit*.

"You wouldn't believe the time I had getting a picture of you, boy. Had to bribe one out of the Triton Special Services Department. That quick change bit. Great gimmick. Just great!" The Hawk sat down next to me and dropped his hand on my knee. "Wonderful place you got here. I like it, like it a lot." Small bones in veined dough. "But not enough to make you an offer on it yet. You're learning fast there, though. I can tell you're learning fast. I'm going to be proud to be able to say I was the one who gave you your first big break." His hand came away and he began to knead it onto the other. "If you're going to move into the big time, you have to have at least one foot planted firmly on the right side of the law. The whole idea is to make yourself indispensable to the good people; once that's done, a good crook has the keys to all the treasure houses in the system. But I'm not telling you anything you don't already know."

"Arty," I said, "do you think the two of us should be seen together here . . . ?"

The Hawk held his hand above his lap and joggled it with a deprecating motion. "Nobody can get a picture of us. I got my men all around. I never go anywhere in public without my security. Heard you've been looking into the security business yourself," which was true. "Good idea. Very good. I like the way you're handling yourself."

"Thanks. Arty, I'm not feeling too hot this evening. I came out here to get some air. . . ."

Arty's hand fluttered again. "Don't worry, I won't hang around. You're right. We shouldn't be seen. Just passing by and wanted to say hello. Just hello." He got up. "That's all." He started down the steps.

"Arty?"

He looked back.

"Sometime soon you will come back; and that time you will want to buy out my share of The Glacier, because I'll have gotten too big; and I won't want to sell because

I'll think I'm big enough to fight you. So we'll be enemies for a while. You'll try to kill me. I'll try to kill you."

On his face, first the frown of confusion; then, the indulgent smile. "I see you've caught on to the idea of hologramic information. Very good. Good. It's the only way to outwit Maud. Make sure all your information relates to the whole scope of the situation. It's the only way to outwit me too." He smiled, started to turn, but thought of something else. "If you can fight me off long enough, and keep growing, keep your security in tiptop shape, eventually we'll get to the point where it'll be worth both our whiles to work together again. If you can just hold out, we'll be friends again. Someday. You just watch. Just wait."

"Thanks for telling me."

The Hawk looked at his watch. "Well. Goodbye." I thought he was going to leave finally. But he glanced up again. "Have you got the new Word?"

"That's right," I said. "It went out tonight. What is it?"

The Hawk waited till the people coming down the steps were gone. He looked hastily about, then leaned towards me with hands cupped at his mouth, rasped, "Pyrite," and winked hugely. "I just got it from a gal who got it direct from Colette" (one of the three Singers of Triton). Then he turned, jounced down the steps, and shouldered his way into the crowds passing on the strip.

I sat there mulling through the year till I had to get up and walk. All walking does to my depressive moods is add the reinforcing rhythm of paranoia. By the time I was coming back, I had worked out a dilly of a delusional system: The Hawk had already begun to weave some security ridden plot about me which ended when we were all trapped in some dead end alley, and trying to get aid I called out, "Pyrite!" which would turn out not to be the Word at all but served to identify me for the man in the dark gloves with the gun/grenades/gas.

There was a cafeteria on the corner. In the light from the window, clustered over the wreck by the curb was a bunch of nasty-grimies (á la Triton: chains around the wrist, bumblebee tattoo on cheek, high heel boots on those who could afford them). Straddling the smashed head-

146

light was the little morph-head I had ejected earlier from The Glacier.

On a whim I went up to her. "Hey?"

She looked at me from under hair like trampled hay, eyes all pupil.

"You get the new Word yet?"

She rubbed her nose, already scratch red. "Pyrite," she said. "It just came down about an hour ago."

"Who told you?"

She considered my question. "I got it from a guy who says he got it from a guy who came in this evening from New York who picked it up there from a Singer named Hawk."

The three grimies nearest made a point of not looking at me. Those further away let themselves glance.

"Oh," I said. "Oh. Thanks."

Occam's Razor, along with any real information on how security works, hones away most such paranoia. Pyrite. At a certain level in my line of work, paranoia's just an occupational disease. At least I was certain that Arty (and Maud) probably suffered from it as much as I did.

The lights were out on The Glacier's marquee. Then I remembered what I had left inside and ran up the stairs.

The door was locked. I pounded on the glass a couple of times, but everyone had gone home. And the thing that made it worse was that I could see it sitting on the counter of the coatcheck alcove under the orange bulb. The steward had probably put it there, thinking I might arrive before everybody left. Tomorrow at noon Ho Chi Eng had to pick up his reservation for the Marigold Suite on the Interplanetary Liner *The Platinum Swan,* which left at one-thirty for Bellona. And there behind the glass doors of The Glacier, it waited with the proper wig, as well as the epicanthic folds that would halve Mr. Eng's sloe eyes of jet.

I actually thought of breaking in. But the more practical solution was to get the hotel to wake me at nine and come in with the cleaning man. I turned around and started down the steps; and the thought struck me, and made me terribly sad, so that I blinked and smiled just from reflex; it was probably just as well to leave it there till morning, because there was nothing in it that wasn't mine, anyway.

Theodore Sturgeon was the guest of honor at the 1962 World Science Fiction Convention in Chicago, in acknowledgment of highly distinguished contributions to our field begun in 1939; but the story below is the first of his to be published— the first new one, anyhow—in a science fiction magazine since then. But it shows, from the title on, that he has lost none of his lifelong interest in the many possible definitions of love; and the voting shows that the past mastery has not been lost, either.

THE MAN WHO LEARNED LOVING

Theodore Sturgeon

His name was Mensch; it once was a small joke between them, and then it became a bitterness. "I wish to God I could have you now the way you were," she said, "moaning at night and jumping up and walking around in the dark and never saying why, and letting us go hungry and not caring how we lived or how we looked. I used to bitch at you for it, but I never minded, not really. I held still for it. I would've, just for always, because with it all you did your own thing, you were a free soul."

"I've always done my own thing," said Mensch, "and I did so tell you why."

She made a disgusted sound. "Who could understand all that?" It was dismissal, an old one; something she had recalled and worked over and failed to understand for years, a thing that made tiredness. "And you used to love people—really love them. Like the time that kid wiped out the fire-hydrant and the street-light in front of the house and you fought off the fuzz and the schlock lawyer and the ambulance and everybody, and got him to the hospital and wouldn't let him sign the papers because he was dazed. And turning that cheap hotel upside down to find Victor's false teeth and bring them to him after they put him in jail. And sitting all day in the waiting room the time Mrs. What's-her-name went for her first throat cancer treatment, you didn't even know her. There wasn't anything you wouldn't do for people."

"I've always done what I could. I didn't stop."

Scorn. "So did Henry Ford. Andrew Carnegie. The Krupp family. Thousands of jobs, billions in taxes for everybody. I know the stories."

"My story's not quite the same," he said mildly.

Then she said it all, without hate or passion or even much emphasis; she said in a burnt-out voice, "We loved each other and you walked out."

They loved each other. Her name was Fauna; it once was a small joke between them. Fauna the Animal and Mensch the Man, and the thing they had between them. "Sodom is a-cumen in," he misquoted Chaucer. "Lewd sing cuckold," (because she had a husband back there somewhere amongst the harpsichord lessons and the mildewed unfinished hooked rugs and the skeleton of a play and all the other abandoned projects in the attic of her life). She didn't get the reference. She wasn't bright—just loving. She was one of those people who waits for the right thing to come along and drops all others as soon as she finds out they aren't the main one. When someone like that gets the right thing, it's forever, and everyone says, my how you've changed. She hasn't changed.

But when the right thing comes along, and it doesn't work out, she'll never finish anything again. Never.

They were both very young when they met and she had a little house back in the woods near one of those resort towns that has a reputation for being touristy-artsy-craftsy and actually does have a sprinkling of real artists in and around it. Kooky people are more than tolerated in places like that providing that a) they attract, or at least do not repel, the tourists and b) they never make any important money. She was a slender pretty girl who liked to be naked under loose floor-length gowns and take care of sick things as long as they couldn't talk—broken-wing birds and philodendrons and the like—and lots of music—lots of *kinds* of music; and cleverly doing things she wouldn't finish until the real thing came along. She had a solid title to the little house and a part-time job in the local frame shop; she was picturesque and undemanding and never got involved in marches and petitions and the like. She just believed in being kind to everyone around her, and thought . . . well, that's not quite right. She hadn't ever thought it out all the way, but she *felt* that if you're kind to everyone the kindness will somehow spread over the world like a healing stain, and that's what you do about wars and greed and injustice. So she was an acceptable, almost approved fixture in the town even when they paved her dirt road and put the lamp-post and fire-hydrant in front of it.

Mensch came into this with long hair and a guitar strapped to his back, a head full of good books and a lot of very serious restlessness. He knew nothing about loving and Fauna taught him better than she knew. He moved in with Fauna the day after she discovered his guitar was tuned like a lute. He had busy hands too, and a way of finishing what he started, yes, and making a dozen more like them—beautifully designed kitchen pads for shopping lists made out of hand-rubbed local woods, which used adding-machine rolls and had a hunk of hacksaw-blade down at the bottom so you could neatly tear off a little or a lot, and authentic reproductions of fireplace bellows and apple-peelers and stuff like that which could be displayed in the shoppes (not stores, they were shoppes) on the village green, and bring in his share. Also he knew about transistors and double-helical gears and eccentric linkages and things like Wankels and fuel-cells. He fiddled around a lot in the back room with magnets and axles and colored fluids of various kinds, and one day he had an idea and began fooling with scissors and cardboard and some metal parts. It was mostly frame and a rotor, but it was made of certain things in a certain way. When he put it together the rotor began to spin, and he suddenly understood it. He made a very slight adjustment and the rotor, which was mostly card-board, uttered a shrill rising sound and spun so fast that the axle, a ten-penny nail, chewed right through the cardboard bearings and the rotor took off and flew across the room, showering little unglued metal bits. He made no effort to collect the parts, but stood up blindly and walked into the other room. Fauna took one look at him and ran to him and held him: what is it? what's the matter? but he just stood there looking stricken until the tears began rolling down his cheeks. He didn't seem to know it.

That was when he began moaning suddenly in the middle of the night, jumping up and walking around in the dark. When she said years later that he would never tell her why, it was true, and it wasn't, because what he told her was that he had something in his head so important that certain people would kill him to get it, and certain other people would kill him to suppress it, and that he wouldn't tell her what it was because he loved her and didn't want her in danger. She cried a lot and said he didn't trust her, and he said he did, but he wanted to take care of her, not throw her to the wolves. He also said—and this is what the moaning and night-walking was all about—that the thing in his head could make the deserts bloom and could feed hungry people all over the world, but that if he let it loose it could be like a plague too, not because of what it was but because of what people would do with it; and the very first person who died because of it would die because of him, and he couldn't bear the idea of that. He really had a choice to make, but before he could make it he had to decide whether the death of one person was too great a price to pay for the happiness and security of millions, and then if the deaths of a thousand would be justified if it meant the end of poverty for all. He knew history and psychology and he had a mathematician's head as well as those cobbler's hands, and he knew damned well what would happen if he took this way or that. For example, he knew where he could unload the idea and all responsibility for it for enough money to keep him and Fauna—and a couple hundred close friends, if it came to that—in total luxury for the rest of their lives; all he would have to do would be to sign it away and see it buried forever in a corporate vault, for there were at least three industrial giants which would urgently bid against one another for the privilege.

Or kill him.

He also thought of making blueprints and scattering millions of copies over cities all over the world, and of finding good ethical scientists and engineers and banding them together into a firm which would manufacture and license the device and use it only for good things. Well you can do that with a new kind of rat-killer or sewing machine, but not with something so potent that it will change the face of the earth, eliminate hunger, smog, and the rape of raw materials—not when it will also eliminate the petrochemical industry (except for dyes and plastics), the electric power companies, the internal combustion engine and everything involved in making it and fuelling it, and even atomic energy for most of its purposes.

Mensch tried his very best to decide not to do anything at all about it, which was the moaning and night-walking interval and that just wouldn't work—the thing would not let him go. Then he decided what to do, and what he must do in order to do it. His first stop was at the town barbershop.

Fauna held still for this and for his getting a job at Flextronics, the town's light industry, which had Government contracts for small computer parts and which was scorned by the town's art, literary and library segment. The regular hours appalled her, and although he acted the same (he certainly didn't look the same) around the house, she became deeply troubled. She had never seen so much money as he brought in every payday, and didn't want to, and for the first time in her life had to get stubborn about patching and improvising and doing without instead of being able to blame poverty for it. The reasons she found now for living that way seemed specious even to her, which only made her stubborn about it, and more of a kook than ever. Then he bought a car, which seemed to her an immorality of sorts.

What tore it was when somebody told her he had gone to the town board meeting, which she had never done, and had proposed that the town pass ordinances against sitting on the grass on the village green, playing musical instruments on town thoroughfares, swimming at the town swimming hole after sundown, and finally, hiring more police. When she demanded an explanation he looked at her sadly for a long time, then would not deny it, would not discuss it, and moved out.

He got a clean room in a very square boarding house

152

near the factory, worked like hell until he got his college credits straightened out, went to night school until he had another degree. He took to hanging around the Legion post on Saturday nights and drank a little beer and bought a lot of whiskey for other people. He learned a whole portfolio of dirty jokes and dispensed them carefully, two-thirds sex, one-third bathroom. Finally he took a leave of absence from his job, which was, by this time, section manager, and moved down the river to a college town where he worked full time on a post-graduate engineering degree while going to night school to study law. The going was very tough around then because he had to pinch every nickel to be able to make it and still keep his pants creased and his brown shoes shiny, which he did. He still found time to join the local church and became a member of the vestry board and a lay preacher, taking as his text the homilys from *Poor Richard's Almanac* and delivering them (as did their author) as if he believed every word.

When it was time he redesigned his device, not with cardboard and glue, but with machined parts that were 70% monkey-puzzle—mechanical motions that cancelled each other, and wiring which energized coils which shorted themselves out. He patented parts and certain groupings of parts, and finally the whole contraption. He then took his degrees and graduate degrees, his published scholarly papers, his patents and his short hair-cut, together with a letter of introduction from his pastor, to a bank, and borrowed enough to buy into a failing company which made portable conveyor belts. His device was built into the drive segment, and he went on the road to sell the thing. It sold very well. It should. A six-volt automobile battery would load coal with that thing for a year without needing replacement or recharging, and no wonder, because the loading was being powered by that little black lump in the drive segment, which, though no bigger than a breadbox, and requiring no fuel, would silently and powerfully spin a shaft until the bearings wore out.

It wasn't too long before the competition was buying Mensch's loaders and tearing them down to see where all that obscene efficiency was coming from. The monkey-puzzle was enough to defeat most of them, but one or two bright young men, and a grizzled oldster or so were able to realize that they were looking at something no bigger than a breadbox which would turn a shaft indefinitely without fuel, and to wonder what things would be likely with this gadget under the hood of a car or in the nacelles of aircraft, or pumping water in the desert, or generating light and power 'way back in the hills and jungles without having to build roads or railways or to string powerlines. Some of these men found their way to Mensch. Either he hired them and tied them up tight with ropes of gold and fringe benefits, or had them watched and dissuaded, or discredited, or, if need be, ruined.

Inevitably someone was able to duplicate the Mensch effect, but by that time Mensch had a whole office building full of lawyers with their pencils sharpened and their instructions ready. The shrewd operator who had duplicated the effect, and who had sunk everything he had and could borrow into retooling an engine factory for it, found himself in such a snarl of infringement, torts, ceases-and-desists, and prepaid royalty demands that he sold his plant at cost to Mensch and gratefully accepted a job managing it. And he was only the first.

The military moved in at about this point, but Mensch was ready for them and their plans to take over his patents and holdings as a national resource. He let himself be bunted higher and higher in the chain of command, while his refusals grew stronger and the threats greater and greater, until he emerged at the top in the company of the civilian who commanded them all. This meeting was brought about by a bishop, for never in all these busy years did Mensch overlook his weekly duty at the church of his choice, nor his tithes, nor his donations of time for an occasional Vacation Bible School or picnic or bazaar. And Mensch, on this pinnacle of wealth, power and respectability, was able to show the President the duplicate set of documents he had placed in a Swiss bank, which on the day his patents were pre-empted by the military, would donate them to research institutes in Albania and points north and east. That was the end of that.

The following year a Mensch-powered car won the Indy. It wasn't as fast as the Granatelli entry; it just voomed around and around the brickyard without making any stops at all. There was, of course, a certain amount of static for a while, but the inevitable end was that the automobile industry capitulated, and with it the fossil-fuel people. Electric light and power had to follow and, as the gas and steam and diesel power sources obsolesce and are replaced by Mensch prime-movers, the atomic plants await their turn.

It was right after the Indianapolis victory that Mensch donated his blueprints to Albania anyway—after all, he had never said he wouldn't—and they showed up about the same time in Hong Kong and quickly reached the mainland. There was a shrill claim from the Soviet Union that the Mensch Effect had been discovered in the 19th century by Siolkovsky, who had set it aside because he was more interested in rockets, but even the Russians couldn't keep that up for long without laughing along with the audience, and they fell to outstripping all other nations in development work. No monkey-puzzle on earth can survive this kind of effort—monkey-puzzles need jungles of patent law to live and thrive—and it was not long before the Soviets (actually, it was a Czech scientist, which is the same thing, isn't it? Well, the Soviets said it was) were able to proclaim that they had improved and refined the device to a simple frame supporting one moving part, the rotor, each made, of course, of certain simple substances which, when assembled, began to work. It was, of course, the same frame and rotor with which Mensch, in terror and tears, had begun his career, and the Czech, that is, Soviet "refinement" was, like all else, what he had predicted and aimed himself toward.

For now there wasn't a mechanics' magazine in the world, nor hardly a tinkerer's workshop anywhere, that didn't begin turning out Mensch rotors. Infringements occurred so widely that even Mensch's skyscraper-full of legal-eagles couldn't have begun to stem the flood. And indeed they did not try, because—

For the second time in modern history (the first was an extraordinary man named Kemal Ataturk) a man of true national-dictator stature set his goal, achieved it, and abdicated. It didn't matter one bit to Mensch that the wiser editorialists, with their knowledgeable index fingers placed alongside their noses, were pointing out that he had defeated himself, shattered his own empire by

155

extending its borders, and that by releasing his patents into the public domain he was making an empty gesture to the inevitable. Mensch knew what he had done, and why, and what other people thought of it just did not matter.

"What does matter," he said to Fauna in her little house by the old fire-hydrant and the quaint street-lamp, "is that there isn't a kraal in Africa or a hamlet in Asia that can't pump water and plow land and heat and light its houses by using a power plant simple enough to be built by any competent mechanic anywhere. There are little ones to rock cradles and power toys and big ones to light whole cities. They pull trains and sharpen pencils, and they need no fuel. Already desalted Mediterranean water is pouring into the northern Sahara; there'll be whole new cities there, just as there were five thousand years ago. In ten years the air all over the earth will be measurably cleaner, and already the demand for oil is down so much that offshore drilling is almost completely stopped. 'Have' and 'have-not' no longer means what it once meant, because everyone has access to cheap power. And that's why I did it, don't you see?" He really wanted very much to make her understand.

"You cut your hair," she said bitterly. "You wore those awful shoes and went to church and got college degrees and turned into a—a typhoon."

"Tycoon," he corrected absently. "Ah, but Fauna, listen: I wanted to be listened to. The way to get what I wanted was short hair, was brown shoes, was published post-graduate papers, was the banks and businesses and government and all of those things that were already there for me to use."

"You didn't need all that. I think you just wanted to move things and shake things and be in the newspapers and history books. You could've made your old motor right here in this house and showed it to people and sold it and stayed here and played the lute, and it would have been the same thing."

"No, there you're wrong," said Mensch. "Do you know what kind of a world we live in? We live in a world where, if a man came up with a sure cure for cancer, and if that man were found to be married to his sister, his neighbors would righteously burn down his house and all his notes.

156

If a man built the most beautiful tower in the country, and that man later begins to believe that Satan should be worshipped, they'll blow up his tower. I know a great and moving book written by a woman who later went quite crazy and wrote crazy books, and nobody will read her great one any more. I can name three kinds of mental therapy that could have changed the face of the earth, and in each one the men who found it went on to insane Institutes and so-called religions and made fools of themselves —dangerous fools at that—and now no one will look at their really great early discoveries. Great politicians have been prevented from being great statesmen because they were divorced. And I wasn't going to have the Mensch machine stolen or buried or laughed at and forgotten just because I had long hair and played the lute. You know, it's easy to have long hair and play the lute and be kind to people when everyone else around is doing it. It's a much harder thing to be the one who does something first, because then you have to pay a price, you get jeered at and they shut you out."

"So you joined them," she accused.

"I used them," he said flatly. "I used every road and path that led to where I was going, no matter who built it or what it was built for."

"And you paid your price," she all but snarled. "Millions in the banks, thousands of people ready to fall on their knees if you snap your fingers. Some price. You could have had love."

He stood up then and looked at her. Her hair was much thinner now, but still long and fine. He reached for it, lifted some. It was white. He let it go.

He thought of fat Biafran babies and clean air and un-polluted beaches, cheaper food, cheaper transportation, cheaper manufacturing and maintenance, more land to lessen the pressure and hysteria during the long slow process of population control. What had moved him to deny himself so much, to rebel, to move and shake and shatter the status quo the way he had, rather than conforming—conforming!—to long hair and a lute? *You could have had love.*

"But I did," he said; and then, knowing she would never, could never understand, he got in his silent fuelless car and left.

Darko Suvin is currently Professor of English at McGill University in Montreal, but was born in Zagreb, Yugoslavia, a linguistic crossroad of the world where he emerged from Serbo-Croat and other Slavic languages to become fluent also in French, German, and Italian—and a specialist in science-fiction history and criticism, seen from the point of view of the main currents of Western philosophy. We have come a long way to have gained such a friend; perhaps someday we shall also be able to say that we have earned him.

THE SF NOVEL IN 1969

D. Suvin

Writing about "the Science Fiction novel" of 1969 one must start by defining one's terms—such as SF—and particularly what they exclude. There is no way around a critical Credo about this genre, buried as it is in a genealogical jungle. All the bleached bones of foolhardy explorers trying to arrive at a definition of SF cannot obviate the necessity of trying to cut through this jungle, in order to arrive within sight of the Sleeping Beauty of SF.

Whatever else it might also be, SF is the *literature of cognitive estrangement*. If we envisage a spectrum of literary subject-matter, running from the ideal extreme of

---

[1] The final nominees for the Nebula Award were: John Brunner, *The Jagged Orbit;* Ursula Le Guin, *The Left Hand of Darkness;* Robert Silverberg, *Up the Line;* Norman Spinrad, *Bug Jack Barron;* Kurt Vonnegut, *Slaughterhouse 5;* and Roger Zelazny, *Isle of the Dead.* Due to a mail strike in Montreal, Silverberg's book did not reach me in time for this essay.

an exact reaction of the author's empirical environment to an exclusive interest in a strange newness, then the literary mainstream of Euro-American civilization had from the eighteenth to the twentieth century been nearer to the first of the two above-mentioned extremes. But at other times, the concern with the domestication of the amazing has been stronger. Early stories about amazing voyages into the next valley—where dog-headed people were found, and also good rock salt which could be taken or at the worst bartered for—catered to hopeful or fearful curiosity about the unknown beyond the next mountain range (sea, ocean, solar system . . .). In them, the thrill of knowledge joined the thrill of adventure. An island in the far-off ocean—including the ether ocean—or a valley beyond the mountain range became the goal of the SF voyage: the sparkling island/valley of Terrestrial Paradise and the dark island/valley of the Dead are both already in folk tales and *Gilgamesh*. Verne's island of Captain Nemo or Wells' valley of the *Country of the Blind* are still within the liberating tradition which contends that the world is not necessarily the way our present empirical island/valley happens to be, and that whoever thinks *his* island/valley is the world, is blind.

The approach to the imaginary locality practiced by the genre of SF is a supposedly factual one: taking off from a fictional ("literary") hypothesis, SF develops it with cognitive ("scientific") rigor. The factual reporting of fictions confronts a set normative system, a closed world picture, with a point of view implying a new set of norms. In literary theory, this is known as the attitude of *estrangement*. This concept was first developed by the Russian Formalists (Viktor Shklovsky), and most successfully underpinned by an anthropological and historical approach in the work of Bertolt Brecht. While working on a play about the prototype scientist Galileo, he defined this attitude in his *Short Organon for the Theatre:* "A representation which estranges is one which allows us to recognize its subject, but at the same time makes it seem unfamiliar." For somebody to see all "normal" happenings in a dubious light, "he would need to develop that detached eye with which the great Galileo observed a swinging chandelier. He was amazed by that pendulum motion as if he had not expected it and could not understand its occurring, and this enabled him to come at the rules by which it was governed." Thus, this look of estrangement is both cognitive and creative, and "one cannot simply exclaim that such an attitude pertains to science, but not to art." Why should not art, in its own way, also contribute to the great social task of furthering Life?

In SF, the attitude of estrangement has become the *formal framework* of the genre. I have argued elsewhere at some length that SF should therefore be defined as *a literary genre whose necessary and sufficient conditions are the presence and interaction of estrangement and cognition, and whose main formal device is an imaginative framework alternative to the author's empirical environment.*

This definition entails some rather clear consequences. If the approach of estrangement differentiates SF from the "realistic" literary mainstream of the eighteenth to twentieth century, its nucleus of cognition differentiates it with equal decisiveness from myth, the fairy tale and the horror fantasy. Based on a lenient interpretation of these criteria, and on available bibliographies, I have calculated that about 160 novels first published in the U.S. in 1969 might qualify as SF. This includes borderline political SF, but excludes sword-and-sorcery fiction and most, though not all, "juvenile" and "sex" SF as being respectively fantasy, juvenile fiction and pornography using some SF trappings for mimicry.

Obviously, this domain of 160 novels is both too large and too narrow for this essay's title. It is too narrow because it does not include other countries—most notably, some British SF novels not published simultaneously in the U.S., and Russian SF: my tries to lay hands on some of the 10–20 SF novels published yearly in the U.S.S.R. in time for this essay unfortunately failed. On the other hand, the domain is too large because it includes a number of pseudo-novels which are really long stories (for example, many Ace Doubles), or collections of stories provided with a frame (for example Fred Saberhagen's *Brother Assassin*); but more to the point because I have not managed to read anywhere near 160 novels. Yet as a sampling of salient tendencies, which was both random (by availability) and weighted (by nominations for Nebula awards), I think it will do.

With these presuppositions explained, one can try to make sense out of the 1969 SF novel. If SF is a genre with a field of possibilities of its own, the criterion of excellence in it is—beside the one of basic literary competence—how close any work comes to using its specific possibilities. In that respect, most of Roger Zelazny's writing is eclectic mythological fantasy and not SF. If we discard metaphors like "SF is the mythology of a technical age" and similar pourings of new wine into old bottles, mythical estrangement is a ritual and religious approach diametrically opposed to SF. Where SF sees the norms of any age, including emphatically its own, as unique, imperfect, changeable, and subject to a *cognitive* glance, myth conceives men's relationships to other men and to nature as fixed and supernaturally—i.e. noncognitively—determined. Where myth claims to explain once and for all the essence of phenomena, SF posits them first as problems and then explores where they lead to; it sees the mythological static identity as an illusion, and usually as a fraud. Thus, to dig into religious archeology for relationships between Egyptian, Greek, Buddhist or other deities, and then to transfer these relationships to a setting midway between Lovecraft and SF, may in the hands of Zelazny's effortless verbal craftsmanship provide some euphoria for teenage readers, which one surely should not begrudge. But his *Isle of the Dead* is clearly strained by the basic incompatibility between the mythical plot and the SF setting and tone. On the one hand, there is an attempt at cognitively explained SF gimmicks such as longevity, planet-forming and personality-recall tapes in the stock van Vogt manner. On the other hand, the underlying conflict of the novel is built on a combination of, I guess, Voodoo deities and a classical Hellenic nether world. I do not mind Voodoo deities in Andre Norton, but it will not do to have them switching their human incarnations erratically in mid-plot for some (symbolistically unclear) needs of Zelazny's, and then try to cover up for it by "realistic", cognitive, SF hints. A spaceship-and-sorcery fantasy, possibly interesting to those who like to sympathize with that sort of thing, is thus contaminated with possibly fine SF, to the detriment of both. Yet this unresolved opposition is perhaps clearer here than in earlier works by Zelazny. Maybe such hesitation means

161

that he might soon openly opt for either fantasy or SF, which one could only welcome.

To my chagrin, I found similar discrepancies, only stronger, in Philip Dick's *Galactic Pot-Healer,* which after a standard anti-utopian beginning flounders to a stop in fairly second-hand symbolistic fantasy (the sunken cathedral etc.), and in Michael Moorcock's *The Black Corridor,* though the latter comes near to validating his "spaceship-universe" situation by the ingenious trick of narration through a paranoiac stream-of-consciousness. Finally, both novels are cop-outs as cognitive SF—or they are fantasy rather than SF. To my mind, these alternatives are synonymous; but even if one does not share this point of view, the lumping of fantasy which reduces all possible horizons to Death into the same category with SF appears as a sociopathological phenomenon of the present moment of "western" culture, and as a grave disservice to SF (and possibly to adult, Kafkaian fantasy too).

At the opposite end—but extremes sometimes meet—is Kurt Vonnegut, Jr.'s, *Slaughterhouse 5,* which draws together various preoccupations from a number of his earlier novels. By devices like making their main characters into marginal characters in this novel, Vonnegut tries to shape a fictional universe of its own—a trick stemming from Balzac (or indeed any coherent mythology) through a great number of others, including SF writers. What powers —gods or laws—rule the Vonnegutian universe? As nearly as one can make out, a sardonic Chance caring exceedingly little for human values. His heroes—here Billy Pilgrim— accept what it brings factually, but remain stoically removed from its absurdities. The privileged Vonnegutian protagonist is an observer, existing in his own imaginative time, who walks through life's horrors like a Dostoevskian Idiot, opposing to it a weary resilience. Billy Pilgrim actually ends up in an American Valhalla, a zoo in another star-system where he is mated with a Hollywood sex-star, and the precognition of which sustains him in his Babbitt-like everyday life (in describing which Vonnegut is at his best).

Ever since *Player Piano,* Vonnegut has been trying to escape SF typing, waxing rather sarcastic about the SF of the 1940's personified for him in "Kilgore Trout" (and having apparently absorbed little SF since). He has in the process made some telling points about life in the SF ghetto, but one wonders whether he hasn't simultaneously spent much ingenuity on building his own ghetto halfway between Sinclair Lewis and Kilgore Trout. I confess I like *Player Piano* better than *Slaughterhouse 5:* it might have been less original, but it was also less weary and certainly no more faddish. Where Paul Porteus could still rebel against Ilium, Billy Pilgrim can only oscillate up-time and down-time from it—an "inner emigration" if there ever was one. On the level of craftsmanship too I fear Vonnegut is becoming repetitive within his canon and even within this novel (e.g. the tag "So it goes" grows increasingly irritating); *Slaughterhouse 5* leaves an impression of thinness compared to the earlier novels. I wish I knew how many Nebula votes were cast for it simply to embarrass the author with an SF prize.

Traditional SF continued extolling individual ingenuity and decency when faced with a hostile set-up (Harry Harrison's *Captive Universe*), or Homo sapiens' ingenuity and toughness when faced with other races (Gordon Dickson's *Wolfling* and *Spacepaw*); or going in for Andersonian sword-and-sorcery-which-is-really-a-superrace's-science (Keith Laumer's *And Now They Wake*). Whether of the liberal, middle-of-the-road, or blood-and-berserker variety, the trouble with this type of SF is that its ethos was fresh and solutions interesting from *A Connecticut Yankee at King Arthur's Court* to the mid-1950's. By now, it has receded—as any *ancien régime* will—into comfortable regions perilously close to fairy tales and juvenile literature. The exciting action is elsewhere, with a group of writers emerging in these last years whom I would like to dub the "New Left" of SF. This has to do with sensibility and world view much more than with personal politics: Delany, a new Brunner and Silverberg come to mind as examples, also a rejuvenated old master —Fritz Leiber, in his much underrated *A Specter Is Haunting Texas*. The common denominator of this rather disparate group is that they question the Individualist ideology, i.e. whether a stable system can be built upon a sum of individual, Robinson-Crusoe greeds as the measure of all values. They are dealing with a post-Berkeley, Vietnam War society of youth revolt, mass media, and big city breakdowns. As different from, say,

Asimov or Pohl and Kornbluth, whose masters of thought were Mill and Spengler in philosophy of history, Dreiser or Sinclair in literature, and Franklin Roosevelt's "fireside chats" on the radio—they deal with their changed environment in a perceptive form for which Joyce, Dos Passos, Malraux, Faulkner, Brecht and intermedia in art, or Marcuse and Mao in philosophy of history, have already happened.

Bug Jack Barron explicates this tendency most immediately. It has the "New Left" intoxication with verbal interfaces and the cynical look at power realities (Bester blazed these trails), the touchingly naive post-*Lady-Chatterley* scenes of sex as the last refuge from the wicked world, the confusion between social regeneration and perceptive reorientation, and so on. It is not only Jack Barron's life which is wrapped up in his mammoth TV-show; the disenchanted, "baby Bolshevik" politics of the book finally also float off into game theory and showbiz rather than into revolutionary action. There is undeniable power in the central strand of the book, the account of Jack Barron's oscillation between the love-game and the power-game in a world of tigers. There is also some overwriting and a characteristically faulty ending. But Spinrad has managed to transfer the "baby Bolshevik" atmosphere into SF; he has significantly contributed to restating the central preoccupation of SF with emerging human relationships in terms of the present young generation.

John Brunner's *The Jagged Orbit* does something similar in terms of a cooler, more European and constructivistic tradition, with "camera eye" sequences rather than formless overflows of impulses. He also postulates a U.S. of the near future which has rejected rationality and cut off the Blacks in segregated "Bantustans", but his political economics of corporate power are far sounder than Spinrad's Faulknerian melodrama of titanic heels. Brunner's protagonist is "the socialization of paranoia" rather than one outstanding character. Instead of the self-questioning of radical Individualism, he portrays the breakdown of its ethos "each for himself and the devil take the hindmost" taken to its logical extreme in the mad "mental hygiene" of Elias Mogshack and universal private armament. A seed of rebirth in the final union of Xavier Conroy (neglected reason) and Lyla Clay (abused emotion) is the only hope of overcoming the schizophrenia of humanity vs. society—"Division Street, Earth" as Brunner calls it (a subplot has the same resolution for Matthew and Celia Flamen). Where Spinrad's basic model of the near future is showbiz, Brunner's is a grimmer, and to me more convincing one of a huge armed madhouse, of which showbiz (personified in Mikki Baxendale and Flamen) is just an intensified offshoot. Better planned and less "gutsy" than Spinrad's, Brunner's novel deals with a similar anti-utopian future by a similar refusal to despair.

Thomas Disch's *Camp Concentration* model—a Dantesque underground concentration camp for criminals and political prisoners who are, during a U.S. nuclear and ABC war in Malaysia, used as guinea-pigs for disease-induced mental experiments—is both a deterministic madhouse of "ethically neutral" natural sciences, and the theater for conchie writer Louis Sacchetti's comedy. The inmates perform *Dr. Faustus* as well as a rejuvenation put-on, Sacchetti writes *Auschwitz: A Comedy,* and there is an incomplete rebirth at the end closer to an SF gimmick than to Dante. Except for that, it is a fine piece of work, baroquely convincing in its erudition, poetry, and manic-depressive tone, all of them well motivated by the nature of the experiment. Though Disch declined the Nebula nomination, he must be put right up there with Brunner and Spinrad.

I have remarked that these last three novels have each some defect in the denouement. The impact of the children's glands, the switch in the robot Madison-Gottschalk, the *deus ex machina* "mind reciprocation," are all slapdash devices permitting formal terminations rather than thematic solutions. This collective Achilles' heel cannot be accidental: the outcome of a novel is the time by which puzzles and tergiversations are impossible, the place where truth will out. But the "New Left", though unique in its desperate realization that human politics are everybody's destiny, as a rule still groping for clear ways out from the political mess it is battling. A writer sharing its sensibility to shop around for some improvised, as often as not mystical, way out.

The most memorable novel of the year is Ursula K. Le Guin's *Left Hand of Darkness,* and I am happy that it received the Nebula Best Novel award. It is a parable of coexistence and understanding, both personal and political, told as the illumination of Genly Ai, first envoy of the galactic union to the planet Gethen. By the end of the novel, aided by the courage and insight of his Gethenian partner Estraven, Ai's political problems have become meaningful as personal insights into the dialectics of death and life, darkness and light (light being "the left hand of darkness"). The different social structure and culture of the Gethenians is caused by their bisexuality and monthly sexual cycle with about six days of "heat". These periods of overriding passion—in any of which any individual may, according to influences of mutual attraction, become male of female—alternate thus with longer periods of erotic indifference. There is no rape and no war. Most importantly, there is no male or female role or expectation of it: "One is respected and judged only as a human being." Even the unusually well-trained and well-meaning Ai has great difficulties in accepting this "appalling experience."

This all adds up to a truly civilized parable on human love and trust independent of (though deeply concerned with) maleness or femininity. It is developed through a series of rich and beautifully controlled binary oppositions, operating on all levels of the novel. Any petty personal and political loyalty—including Ai's one to the galactic union—pales before the higher love of humanity: such is the message of the book, condensed in the interpolated little politico-personal legend of Arek and Terem, which one might call the "Romeo and Juliet of Gethen." The deceptive simplicity and lucidity of Mrs. Le Guin's writing matches the quality of human relations shown. Even the opposition between the collectivistic, police-ridden bureaucracy of Orgoreyn and the moody, loose unpredictability of Kerhide which is fast converging with the Orgoreyn model, though slightly suggestive of an U.S.S.R.-U.S. juxtaposition, is far superior to the ugly Cold War sneers of "Us" and "Them" in the manner say, of Laumer's Retief stories. When one compares *The Left Hand of Darkness* with other 1969 offerings on a similar theme, say (in ascending relevance) with A. Bertram Chandler's *Spartan Planet*, Hughes Cooper's *Sexmax*, Edmund Cooper's *The Last Continent*, and even Anne McCaffrey's competent and appealing *Decision at Doona*—

Mrs. Le Guin's qualities blaze forth. In a way, she could be claimed as a major victory of the "New Left" in SF: for a literary stream is really victorious only when it has permeated the center of its genre. Mrs. Le Guin is less flashy and abrasive than the "New Left", but her novel shares their unsentimental warm concern with collective humanism. Saying "yes" to new rather than just "no" to the old values, she is right at the center of SF relevance, allowing us to recognize our central concerns through a detour of estrangement. Her novel speaks—to use her words—to our "strong though undeveloped sense of humanity, of human unity. I got quite excited thinking about this."

Finally, I want to mention a book which I should theoretically dislike, based as it is on astrological metaphors, but which seems too significant to be passed over in silence. This is Piers Anthony's *Macroscope* (Avon), a bulky novel starting from a new instrument of knowledge and expanding into wondrous, almost Stapledonian or Doc-Smith-like adventures of a spaceship crew single-handedly saving the galaxy. If this sounds indigestible, let me say it is served with a bewildering succession of very well-composed sauces derived from the doctrine of correspondences. But the correspondences are followed through with impressive consistence, ingenuity, lyricism and exuberance (too much exuberance, one sighs around page 400). If the book is symbolistic, it is at least vividly and precisely so; and it says some worthwhile things about our savagery and responsibility, personal and collective. The first task of the critic, cutting across any theories he might cherish is still to respond to a powerful imagination. Piers Anthony may be a name to watch—especially should he turn to liberating rather than hierarchical metaphors, to alchemy rather than astrology.

All in all, it has not been a bad year. Compared with the seven lean years after the Sputnik, when only isolated flashes relieved the gloom of Anglophone SF, one could even say that it was rather good. Perhaps we are seeing the beginnings of a widening sense of formal and social urgency, not to mention of some elementary logic. Should such subversive ideas spread, we might even live to see a really good year. Never say die.

Alexei Panshin, who was trained as a librarian, won a Nebula award for his first novel, Rite of Passage (1968), *and is the author of one of our field's few books of authentic literary criticism,* Heinlein in Dimension. *He is thus that rare combination, both creator and scholar, as the following essay shows.*

SHORT SF IN 1968

Alexei Panshin

Recently, with one outstanding exception—science fiction —the short story has fallen on hard times. Thirty years ago the pulps and their grown relatives like *The Saturday Evening Post* published short fiction by the yearly thousands of stories. Today, except for a few stories published in men's and women's specialty magazines, the commercial short story has all but disappeared. The serious short story is largely confined to literary magazines of small circulation.

The causes of the situation are not certain. Conventional wisdom has it that the advent of television was the death of the pulp short story. It is usually said that mindless people turned from one simple entertainment that required them to think to a simpler one that didn't. While this may be partly true, it isn't the whole truth. Simple adventure fiction continues to be written and sold. Pulp novels like Doc Savage are reprinted in paperback and sell excellently. It is just the short story that has disappeared. Television may have been a factor, but it may also be that the pulp short story was an overworked form.

The Saturday Evening Post and *Collier's* apparently had large audiences for the fiction they printed at the time they died. So it is said. Their circulations were high, but they were deserted by advertising. If there is a demand for Post-style fiction, however, it has yet to be taken advantage of by reader-supported magazines, the middle American equivalent of the science fiction magazine. Perhaps an opportunity is being missed.

The literary short story generally dies with its small audience. A few annual anthologies summarize the year and persistent authors earn hardcover collections which sell mainly to libraries. But in the main, the literary short story is written primarily for the author's friends.

The one apparently solid block in all this rubble is science fiction. In 1969, around 350 new short stories were published in American science fiction magazines, up from 300 the year before. More new short stories were published for the first time in anthologies like Robert Silverberg's *Tomorrow's Worlds,* which included one original story among its reprints, or in single-author collections like Harlan Ellison's *The Beast That Shouted Love at the Heart of the World,* the American source of publication for his "A Boy and His Dog." There are now at least five regular or semi-regular anthologies of original stories: Damon Knight's *Orbit* from Putnam and Berkley, Harry Harrison's *Nova* from Dell, Robert Silverberg's *New Dimensions* from Walker and Avon, Chip Delany's *Warp* from Paperback Library and *Infinity* from Robert Hoskins at Lancer. There are the odd anthologies of original stories like those coming from Bova, Ellison, Gerrold, Harrison and Silverberg, to mention only those of which I've heard. And finally, of course, the stray science fiction story is published in Playboy or McCall's. Altogether, there is enough original science fiction published to support two sets of awards and three annual resumé anthologies, including this one, with only a minimum of overlap.

Besides this, there is a large amount of old short science fiction reprinted each year. Not only do Niven and Ellison issue new collections of their magazine fiction, but Heinlein collections that have seen printing after printing continue to be reissued. Similarly, we see both new anthologies and reprints of older anthologies. And the science fiction magazines republished another 175 stories last year.

The trend seems to be toward more short science fiction rather than less. In 1969, two former science fiction magazines were revived, *Spaceways* and *Venture,* and the imminent resurrection of two others, *Worlds of Fantasy* and *Worlds of Tomorrow,* has been advertised. Rather more important is the proliferation of original anthologies. This experiment has been tried before, most notably in Fred Pohl's *Star* series in the fifties, but more commonly anthologies of original stories have been announced but never appeared because of a lack of usable submissions. This no longer seems to be the case. In fact, whether because of freedom from magazine deadlines, freedom from magazines taboos, freedom from any of the regularities of length and content that mark *Analog* or *Galaxy,* or because of the relative freshness of new editorial vision, perhaps not unlike the freshness that Campbell, Boucher and Gold once brought to science fiction, the liveliest SF of recent years has appeared in original anthologies. It is more than coincidence that only one of the last nine Nebula awards for short fiction was given to a story that had first publication in an American science fiction magazine.

As a writer I have no special fondness for the short story. I write novels because the science fiction novel is a nearly unexplored form. In the days of magazine science fiction, novels made up only some five per cent of all SF published, and even today the SF novel is less common than the science fiction short story. When I write short stories, it is as an easy way to start writing after a layoff, or as a change of pace between novels, or as a way of getting rid of a small nagging idea. I would not agree with either Harlan Ellison or Joanna Russ when they say that the short story is science fiction's natural form—it has merely been the most common.

Because I am not entirely sympathetic to it, my wonder at the success of the science fiction short story in these times is all the greater. This success is one of the three most wonderworthy externals of contemporary science fiction. The other two are the sociology of the science fiction audience, which is unique and certainly deserves study, and the extraordinary popular success of *Stranger in a Strange Land* and *Dune* to a degree previously impossible for books published as science fiction.

The endurance of the SF short story is a rare trick, made all the rarer because science fiction is a literature of the strange, the archetypical, and the universal, and it is difficult to talk about these things both briefly and well. New worlds, new characters and new ideas may be invoked, but in the space of one science fiction short story they cannot be lived with, known, examined or exhausted.

The possibilities of complication and development have led one science fiction writer after another to write connected stories, from Heinlein's Future History to Perry Chapdelaine's Spork, the absolute latest of series, begun this past year. Ursula Le Guin's "Winter King" in *Orbit* 5 takes on added meaning and power from its connection to her Nebula winning novel, *The Left Hand of Darkness*. Robert Silverberg's "To Jorslem" is the sequel to two other magazine stories, one of them a Hugo winning novelette; all three have already been published together as a novel, *Nightwings*. Anne McCaffrey's "Dramatic Mission" was part of a series that she has been building since 1961. The interesting thing about these last two stories is that they are both novellas, as though Silverberg and McCaffrey were not content with the scope afforded by a series, but having won themselves elbow room for more.

Mosaics like Le Guin's or McCaffrey's can be fascinating. They are certainly one reason for the existence of short science fiction. There are readers who enjoy following the piece by piece revelation of a strange universe. There is some danger, however, in double purpose. Stories that read well enough individually may not prove to have direction or weight or meaning as a group, or when they do have direction, weight and meaning may seem nothing more than a clumsy way to write a novel, as Silverberg's *Nightwings*.

At the other extreme from the series story lies the visionary fragment, the pure flash of strange that copes with the limitations of the short story by paying lip service only to story or ignoring it altogether. Let us

171

frankly admit that a good many short science fiction stories are not stories at all. Samuel R. Delany's "Time Considered as a Helix of Semi-Precious Stones" is nothing but a bright fragment. This is a weakness, but not a fatal one, not in science fiction. We live by our visions. There are times when a good vision that fits no story can be its own justification. At the least, Delany's fragment, whether truly self-justifying or not, has considerable charm.

The series allows a certain amount of flexibility around limitation. The fragment ignores limitation. Most short science fiction, however, copes with limitation by falling into one of three conventional forms—in a sense, frankly admitting to limitation and then playing on from there.

The triumph-of-knowledge story, once tremendously popular, is now much less common. In its purest form, it poses a melodramatic situation that can only be firmly and finally settled for all time by some strange physical fact known to a few since the twentieth century. It is mainly to be found today in *Analog,* although its best-known contemporary practitioner, Larry Niven, has never appeared in *Analog.* At its best, the story that fingers a small fact and finds it wonderful can be an intense experience and an asset to science fiction. At its absolute worst, however, this sort of story all too often can detail the way in which a heroic figure's private knowledge of dowsing settles the hash of psionic monsters.

Moralities, too, are still written today. Among last year's noted stories, Theodore Sturgeon's "The Man Who Learned Loving" and Norman Spinrad's "The Big Flash" were both morality plays. Both come to terms with the problems of length by stating short moral lessons—that love of mankind is more important than love of an individual, and that modern apocalyptic rock has the power to destroy the world. For stories like these to be effective, not only must the moral be worth drawing, but it must be drawn effectively. And morality play runs the risk of platitude or idiosyncrasy, and of being passed by events. Moralities, no matter how good they may seem at the time they are written, tend not to wear well.

This is not to say that moral questions have no place in science fiction. Science fiction's power to speak of the general case, the universal, makes morality a natural subject. By and large, however, the answers science fiction has proposed to moral questions, particularly in short stories, have been clearly inadequate. Good moral questions don't resolve themselves that easily. On the other hand, some very good short science fiction stories, as for instance Ursula Le Guin's "Nine Lives", cope very satisfactorily with the problems of limitation by raising unusual moral problems, stating them well and resting content.

The last and apparently most durable of the conventional acceptances of limitation is the mousetrap, the cherrybomb, the irony. If the bang at the end is big enough, we are prepared to be charmed by almost any sort of lie. Robert Silverberg's "Passengers" is a beautifully nasty example, and Harlan Ellison's "A Boy and His Dog," while in large part a morality, is also an irony, and the ambivalence seems to add power and tension to the story. However, if these two stories are admirable, it is only in part because their surprises are effective. Surprise as a formal principle stands a good chance of outwearing its welcome. You can be surprised in the same way just so many times before you begin to shrug. This is one reason that stories sometimes seem to run in cycles. One year will be all comic computer stories and the next there will be none.

Fortunately irony is an inexhaustible mode, and even more fortunately writers like Ellison and Silverberg are not satisfied to let irony stand by itself. Good writing is possible in science fiction. What is more important, the sheer impossibility of talking about strange worlds economically while telling a story worth hearing has teased SF writers into marvels of compression. The ability to evoke the strange and new in a few words is a marvelously subtle tool with even more relevance to the science fiction novel than the science fiction short story.

Finally, there are occasions when a science fiction short story quite impossibly transcends limitation and expresses the epitomal. It is this possibility, I think, that keeps the science fiction short story alive, that holds readers when other short story forms cannot, that challenges writers like me who feel they have more urgent business elsewhere to return to the form again and again.

I don't know if any of this year's crop of short science fiction can be said to be epitomal. Grace demands that

173

they age for a few years before we make that kind of judgment. At this moment, what I can safely say is that this year's Nebula winning stories are readable stories and solid credits to science fiction.

NEBULA AWARDS

NEBULA AWARDS 1965

Best Novel: *Dune* by Frank Herbert.
Best Novella: (tie) "The Saliva Tree" by Brian W. Aldiss; "He Who Shapes" by Roger Zelazny.
Best Novelette: "The Doors of His Face, the Lamps of His Mouth" by Roger Zelazny.
Best Short Story: " 'Repent, Harlequin!' Said the Ticktockman" by Harlan Ellison.

NEBULA AWARDS 1966

Best Novel: (tie) *Flowers for Algernon* by Daniel Keyes; *Babel–17* by Samuel R. Delany.
Best Novella: "The Last Castle" by Jack Vance.
Best Novelette: "Call Him Lord" by Gordon R. Dickson.
Best Short Story: "The Secret Place" by Richard McKenna.

NEBULA AWARDS 1967

Best Novel: *The Einstexin Intersection* by Samuel R. Delany.
Best Novella: "Behold the Man" by Michael Moorcock.
Best Short Story: "Aye, and Gomorrah" by Samuel R. Delany

NEBULA AWARDS 1968

Best Novel: *Rite of Passage* by Alexei Panshin.
Best Novella: "Dragonrider" by Anne McCaffrey.
Best Novelette: "Mother to the World" by Richard Wilson.
Best Short Story: "The Planners" by Kate Wilhelm.

NEBULA AWARDS 1969

Best Novel: *The Left Hand of Darkness* by Ursula K. Le Guin.

Best Novella: "A Boy and His Dog" by Harlan Ellison.

Best Novelette: "Time Considered as a Helix of Semi-Precious Stones" by Samuel R. Delany.

Best Short Story: "Passengers" by Robert Silverberg.